An odd musky smell filled the cave. It was familiar, but Jimmy couldn't place it.

Lassie whined from the entrance.

"It's okay, girl," he called back. "I don't think this goes very far."

He walked four strides, then the stone narrowed too much to stand. He knelt and wriggled forward on his knees until the stone squeezed him to a stop. His light beam was narrow and only the size of a penny. But carefully, like a good archaeologist's helper, he swung the little light up and down the walls. Red and brown stone walls without any drawings or etchings flashed in and out of sight. He was glad he hadn't called Uncle Cully over to investigate after all.

He couldn't turn around, so he shrugged back on his knees when a faint scratching stopped him. The noise was in front of him, not behind him where Lassie stood. Lassie whined again behind him.

Do snakes hide in caves? he thought suddenly. He sent the beam across the floor as far back as it would reach. Something moved just beyond the light. A shudder ran down his spine. He crawled backward fast and stood when the stone allowed.

Two beady eyes gleamed in the narrow light. Then the eyes vanished. . . .

D0064226

Lassie™

Danger at
Echo Cliffs

These heartwarming stories of a boy and his beloved dog Lassie have demonstrated the values of faithfulness, loyalty, and love to boys and girls for nearly five decades. As Jimmy and Lassie face different situations through the Lassie stories from Chariot Family Publishing, these same principles will come alive for children of the '90s in a way that they can understand and apply to their lives.

Look for these Lassie books from Chariot
at your local Christian bookstore.

Under the Big Top
Treasure at Eagle Mountain
To the Rescue
Hayloft Hideout
Danger at Echo Cliffs

Danger at
Echo Cliffs

Adapted by
Marian Bray

Chariot Books™
A Division of Cook Communications

Chariot Books™ is an imprint of Chariot Family Publishing
Cook Communications, Colorado Springs, Colorado 80918
Cook Communications, Paris, Ontario
Kingsway Communications, Eastbourne, England

LASSIE™: DANGER AT ECHO CLIFFS
© 1996 by Broadway Video Entertainment, LP, under license from
Palladium Limited Partnership. All rights reserved. Except for brief excerpts
for review purposes, no part of this book may be reproduced or used in any
form without written permission from the publisher.

The trademark LASSIE™ is registered in the United States Patent and
Trademark Office and in other countries. All rights reserved.

Cover illustration by Ron Mazellan
Cover design by Joe Ragont Studios

First Printing, 1996
Printed in United States of America
00 99 98 97 96 5 4 3 2 1

Danger at Echo Cliffs is a Christian adaptation
of characters and situations based on the
Lassie television series. TV scripts are used by
permission of the copyright holder.

Table of Contents

The Adventure Begins

They're here!" ten-year-old Sarah Harmon yelled as she bounded up the stairs. She needed one quick check to make sure she had everything for the week ahead.

As soon as thirteen-year-old Jimmy Harmon heard his sister yell, he dashed to the window of his upstairs bedroom to make sure what she said was true. The familiar sound of his uncle's van horn—*beep, duh-beep, duh-beep, beep, beep*—could be heard throughout the house, charging it with the excitement and electricity that a visit from Uncle Cully always brought.

Lassie, Jimmy's tri-colored, rough coat collie, was doing her usual "I'm so excited" jig about Jimmy's bedroom. Without fully understanding the whole situation, she knew something was about to happen.

Jimmy grabbed the things he had laid out for the trip and headed for the door. Just as he entered the hallway, Sarah ran past him in a blur.

"Beat 'cha down the stairs," she said without stopping.

"Oh, no, you don't!" Jimmy said as he tried to elbow his way past her. They sounded like a herd of elephants rumbling down the stairway.

Lassie knew better than to squeeze between them, so she stayed at the top of the stairs and barked. When the rumbling ended in a laughing pile up at the foot of the stairs, she made her way down, nails clicking on the wooden stairs, and gave Jimmy's face a swipe with her wet tongue.

"Oh, yuk, Lassie," he said, arm raised against her next attack. "You really know how to hurt a guy when he's down."

"I'd say that was a kiss for the winner," Mrs. Harmon said laughingly as she viewed the sight before her.

"Well, I can tell by this display of enthusiasm that everyone is ready for a week of fun and frolic," Uncle Cully said as he walked through the front door. Uncle Cully, who was fifteen years younger than Dad, was always ready for a good time.

"Yeah, right," Jimmy added sarcastically. "Searching for bones and ruins in New Mexico is not my idea of fun and frolic."

"You never know with Uncle Cully," Pastor Paul Harmon said as he walked into the room carrying the morning paper. "He might have some surprises up his sleeve."

At that Paul turned to his brother, "How have you been, Cully?" he asked.

Cully's blue eyes sparkled. "Oh, I'm doing fine," he

responded. "But being an archeology professor has its drawbacks. I really love getting out of the classroom and actually digging. I've been looking forward to this trip for a long time."

"Why don't you come into my study for a minute and we can go over your plan," Dad said. "Just in case you get off the beaten path, I want to know where to start looking." Dad and Uncle Cully stepped inside Dad's office and began looking at the opened map lying on the desk.

As Jimmy and Sarah took their backpacks and sleeping bags out to the van, they saw the five graduate students stretching and doing toe touches to limber up their road-weary bodies.

Soon Mom and Dad and Uncle Cully joined them, and after some brief introductions and several good-byes, Cully sped out of the driveway and headed southwest for New Mexico.

The hours droned on. Occasionally they stopped for breaks and to switch drivers, but their goal was to drive straight through until they reached their destination—no overnighters. It was uncomfortable riding in the van for so long. Sleep made the trip easier.

⚓

Jimmy opened his eyes. The road rumbled smoothly underneath him. Where was he? He looked ahead. He could see Uncle Cully at the driver's seat, silhouetted by the dash lights. Otherwise the moving vehicle was dark and quiet. Outside a nearly full moon raced beside him, lighting up a desert landscape.

Then he remembered. They were on a cool adventure. Uncle Cully had invited Jimmy, Sarah, and Lassie to join him and five of his archeology graduate students from the University of Michigan on a field trip to study some of America's first people, the Anasazi.

"Are we there yet?" Sarah whispered sleepily from the other side of Lassie.

Sarah had asked that same question about fifty million times since they had left home in Farley, Iowa. The rolling farmland of Iowa was about as different from New Mexico as the moon was from the sun.

"Another hour or so," Karina Peña said softly. She was one of the graduate students who sat in the seat directly in front of them.

"Good," said Sarah, snuggling down on Lassie's furry flank. "Wake me when we get to Grandpa's."

Their grandparents, Noel and Lila Owens, were helping outfit Uncle Cully's spring break trip. The Owenses' ranch was between the Laguna Indian reservation and the Cibola National Forest. Grandpa Owens raised Spanish mustangs, and they were going to ride horses for five days through the rugged New Mexican high desert, searching for some of the Anasazi ruins.

Jimmy had always liked dogs better than horses, but he'd rather ride a horse than hike through the desert!

"How come you're awake?" Karina asked Jimmy. He liked all the college students, but especially Karina. She had long black hair and looked like Pocahontas or some other Native American princess.

"I don't know," Jimmy said. "I guess something just told me we were nearly there."

Jimmy could hear the smile in her voice. "I'm from New Mexico, but I still get excited when I come home. It's a place that you can't really ever leave. The desert stays inside you once you've been there."

"I guess so," said Jimmy. "I come almost every summer to visit my grandparents. But I've never been to Little Lizard Canyon before."

"I've been near it," said Karina. "I used to help herd our sheep around the Cebolleta Mountains."

"I think it's about twenty miles from my grandparents' ranch" said Jimmy.

"It's not so much the distance as how the land is."

"How is the land?" asked Jimmy. He thought he knew, after all he'd ridden with Grandpa before—just stretches of sand and sage, gouged earth, and jutting rocks.

"Oh, the land is cruel. Very dry. Mean and tough." Jimmy could hear the smile in her voice again. "But that is how we are, too. Mean and tough, right?"

15

Jimmy laughed.

Sarah said crossly, "Some of us are trying to sleep. It is still night, you know."

"Sorry," said Jimmy, and he and Karina were quiet. Jimmy gazed out the window, his hand on Lassie's soft fur, and in the east a sharp red light outlined the Sandia Mountains.

❦

"See that notch in the mountain?" asked Grandpa Owens the next morning, his calloused hand on the bridle of his grandson's mount. Jimmy knew his grandfather worked hard at everything he did, including caring for his purebred horses. Mom would tease her dad, declaring the horses were as much his babies as she had been.

All of Grandpa and Grandma's Spanish mustangs had mathematical names because Grandpa had taught high school math for years. "Can't get the numbers and formulas out of my head" Grandpa would say.

Concentrate, Jimmy told himself as he squinted, staring along Grandpa's arm and pointing finger to the distant mountain range. Under him, Geometry, a silver-colored mustang, pawed her front leg. Let's go! she was saying. Enough of this looking around. Let's go have an adventure!

The Cebolleta mountain line dipped and rose as Geometry pranced. Jimmy was glad for the western saddle with the horn so he could hold on. He didn't care if cow-

16

boys never touched the horn, he wasn't going to let a horse unload him!

Lassie barked sharply at Jimmy's horse as if to tell her to knock it off, but the mare ignored both Jimmy and Lassie, and pranced in place like a race horse.

Jimmy concentrated on the dark stain of mountains and carefully followed their outline. Wait. There. He did see the notch. One plunge in a series of jagged leaps, then the top ridge had a chunk missing as if a giant monster had taken a bite out of the ridge line.

"Okay, I see it," said Jimmy.

"That's where you're going," said Grandpa. He took the silver horse's headstall and said sternly, "Whoa, Geometry. Stand still." The mare stood for a full half minute before jigging again.

"I wish I were going with you. I really do," Grandpa said.

"I wish you were, too," said Jimmy. He really did. Grandpa had had some surgery, and even though he felt good, he wasn't to do anything vigorous for another month.

"Life is vigorous," he'd said last night, but Grandma threatened to hog-tie him if he even tried to clamber through the ruins on horseback.

So instead of Grandpa as their guide to see the Anasazi ruins, the new farmhand, Decker, was going along with them. Jimmy didn't like him. He seemed, well, slimy. But maybe that was just because he wanted Grandpa to come instead.

Grandpa continued, "And when you come back home, you keep the notch right behind you and the setting sun on your right shoulder."

"What happens if it's cloudy," asked Sarah, "and you can't see the sun?"

Grandpa grinned. "Then you pray, real hard."

Karina sidestepped her gelding, who had zebra-like stripes on his lower legs, and added teasingly, "Don't pray too hard for the clouds to go away," she said. "My people have been praying for rain."

"Well," said Sarah suddenly. "What happens then? Do the prayers ex each other out, like votes?"

Uncle Cully laughed and urged his horse up to Jimmy's.

"There is a middle ground," said Uncle Cully. "Maybe some light rain showers with small clouds?"

Karina tossed her long black hair. "Never a light rain here, Dr. Harmon."

"Now Ms. Peña, remember not to speak in absolutes," said Uncle Cully, and they laughed as if it were an old joke. Jimmy had already noticed a mutual respect between Uncle Cully and Karina. Although Karina had said she was half-Mexican, he thought she looked more like her Indian heritage. Navajo, she'd told them when they introduced themselves. The

18

Navajo word for Navajo was Dinè, meaning *the people.* But she was from the Hopi clan. It was confusing. He hadn't had a chance to ask her to explain.

Grandpa let go of Geometry's bridle and said, "You best be off before this mare digs herself into a hole."

They all started for the gate into the Owenses' upper pasture. Decker held open the gate with his boot, sitting causally on his own horse as if the animal were nothing more than a bicycle. The horse was an ugly creature.

Lassie trotted beside Geometry, taking in the sights all around them, ever watchful. Eight of them rode Grandpa's Spanish mustangs, and Decker rode his dull bay. Two sturdy pack mules had been borrowed from a neighbor. Decker lead the mules and they stood beside the open gate, long ears relaxed.

Jimmy turned in the saddle and waved to Grandpa, who was leaning on the corral fence. Grandma joined him. They waved until the group vanished behind a rise. Ahead surged the high desert, barely subdued by the winter, only slightly gentled in the spring.

When the sun popped above the mountains, their destination, the base of the Cebolleta Mountains, flamed orange and red. Jimmy wanted to gallop to meet them.

Adventure, here I come!

The Notch in the Mountains

As they rode through the morning, great slashes of sunlight fell across the nine riders and their horses. Piñon jays, a type of bird common to the dessert, screamed insults as the riders past the pine trees. Jimmy grinned as a bold jay whooshed over his head like an F-14, chattering and hollering. A twig with a clump of needles fell past Geometry's head. She shied sideways.

"Hey," Jimmy said, after calming the mare, "that jay was bombing me."

"I guess it is his country," said Connor Martin, an African-American from Minnesota. He was taller than Uncle Cully, who was six feet, one inch. Grandpa had given Connor the largest horse. Jimmy liked watching Connor. As big as he was, he was deft with his hands and had helped Grandpa change bits on the bridles for each of the horses.

"It's hot," exclaimed Sarah, taking off her jacket.

"Wait until tonight," Decker called over his narrow shoulder. "Then it'll be freezing."

As they rode the dusty, stony trail, Jimmy watched the notched mountain Grandpa had shown him. The landmark had shifted so it wasn't straight in front of them anymore. It was off to the west. Should he say something?

No, Uncle Cully was too involved with his stuents to notice the notch. Jimmy didn't want to break up what was *really* school for the college students. So he clucked his tongue and Geometry broke into a jog, her silvery mane dancing in the breeze. He passed Sarah and her sorrel alazàn horse, Calculus.

During the summers, Jimmy and Sarah stayed with Grandpa and Grandma. Grandpa had a neat way of teaching information about the detailed colors of his Spanish mustangs with verses from the Bible. Jimmy grinned, remembering the verse about the white horse Jesus will ride at the head of the armies of God.

Grandpa would demand, "What color of white horse?" Jimmy knew very few horses were truly white. "Is the horse a *perlino, isabella, cremello?* Or a light gray or a claybank dun?" Jimmy couldn't think of any other near-white colors, but he knew Grandpa would be able to fire off a half a dozen others and would get after him for not knowing more.

He chuckled, realizing for the first time that Grandpa was assuming that the heavenly horses would be Spanish mustangs.

Jimmy missed having Grandpa with them.

Geometry flattened her ears as they approached the mules trailing Decker and his horse. Jimmy wondered why Decker didn't ride one of Grandpa's horses. Of his own horse, Decker had said, "Picked him up cheap at a rodeo." Jimmy could imagine someone getting rid of a lousy horse cheap.

"What's up?" asked Decker. He lazily swung the mules' lead line like a kids' jump rope, back and forth.

Lassie, back from investigating some interesting scent, trotted up between Jimmy's and Decker's horses. Jimmy wasn't sure if his dog were intentionally getting between himself and Decker, but it had happened several times before they had ever started riding this morning. Lassie never growled at Decker, but Jimmy had a feeling his collie was uneasy with the man.

Suddenly Decker's horse kicked at Lassie.

Jimmy yelled, making Geometry spook off the trail. She stumbled into bright red desert paintbrush flowers and nearly went into a patch of strawberry cactus. Lassie, however, had sensed the brown horse bunching his muscles and dodged the lightning kick.

"He kicks dogs," said Decker.

"Thanks for the warning," said Jimmy dryly and urged Geometry back onto the trail. Decker just looked at him questioningly.

"My grandfather told me that we should head straight at that notch in the mountain," Jimmy said, knowing Decker would think he was a dumb kid. But he had to say something.

Decker looked, but didn't say anything. Jimmy's face flushed. Decker had lived around here most of his life. Who was Jimmy to think he had a clue as to where they were going? "I was just wondering why we aren't going in that direction," he said, pointing to the notch.

Decker winked. "Now don't you worry. I used to fish in Little Lizard Canyon. There's a big, deep pool there. There's also hot springs. That water'll feel good after a day in the saddle."

"Okay, well, thanks." Jimmy let Geometry drop back.

After a few minutes of continuing to veer off to the right, he pulled out his compass and took a bearing on the notch. *Just so I have some idea what direction we're going,* he thought. *Besides, it's good practice.*

Taking a bearing while on a moving horse wasn't easy though. He tried to stop Geometry for a minute, but she wouldn't have any of that. The other horses were leaving her and no way was she, a smart little mustang, going to be left alone with some dumb Iowa kid in the desert.

So he did his best and figured at least he'd have some idea of which way was Grandpa's ranch. He glanced over at Mount Taylor, a visual beacon in the south. Karina had pointed out the mountains before they left, telling them that the Navajo called the mountain *Tsoodzil* or Blue Bead Mountain. *Better name,* he thought. The mountain was sacred to Karina and her people. Maybe like Mount Sinai. He'd have to ask Karina what had happened on the the mountain to make it sacred.

Lassie streaked off after something quick and brown. Of course nearly everything around them blurred into some shade of brown. It wasn't like Iowa in the spring, bursting with green.

A large bird wheeled overhead; then without flapping its wings, it soared in a huge circle, around and around and around. He wondered if it were a hawk or even an eagle.

Everything was so different here.

Something floated near Geometry's head. She snorted and rolled an eye. Another round thing floated a little higher. The mare didn't see that one. The sun caught the wet-looking curved rim and sprinkled rainbow colors.

A cluster of them blew across his mare's ears and she snorted again. Bubbles! They were soap bubbles.

Someone laughed and hooves clattered close. It was Petra Elliott. The girl with the New Jersey accent. She blew more bubbles with a small plastic wand. Geometry shied again.

"I guess she's never seen soap bubbles before," said Jimmy.

"They aren't indigenous to the desert regions," said Petra with a grin. She had more freckles than he did! She added, "The look on your face made me think you'd never seen soap bubbles before either!"

"I thought at first they were some kind of seed pod or something."

"She blows bubbles everywhere she goes," said Connor in his baritone voice.

"It's my trademark," explained Petra. The bubbles dashed away on the wind, throwing themselves onto the stern cactus and unyielding piles of stones.

If anyone in Jimmy's middle school blew soap bubbles anywhere, he or she would be the laughing stock of the school. *College sure must be different,* he thought.

Lassie loped back to Geometry's side, her tongue flapping against her chest. Geometry didn't seem to mind the big collie. Jimmy was glad. That could have been a problem. Lassie was careful to steer clear of Decker's ugly horse's heels though.

More bubbles streamed by, and Geometry figured out they were harmless. She ignored them, even when a couple popped on her furry ears. Jimmy patted her firm neck. "Good girl," he was saying proudly when the little mare slammed to a halt and twisted back on her tail. Jimmy, despite his resolution to not be thrown, shot out of the saddle.

Solitario Butte

For a strange, stretched-out moment, Jimmy thought he wasn't going to fall off. He grabbed at Geometry's long mane, but the coarse hair burned across his palms.

He hit the ground. He'd always heard Grandpa say, "If you fall, the ground will catch you." Grandpa's words seemed to hang over him like a shooting star.

Then someone screamed and the fuzzy words vanished. His mouth was full of fur. A jabbing sensation shot up his arm. His left eyebrow spiked pain.

Desert and sky reversed until Lassie's frantic barking turned the world right side up again. He sat up. His dog ran over, putting her paws on his chest, and pushed him back.

"This way, boy," said Decker as he yanked Jimmy to his feet and hauled him farther back.

Sarah shouted Lassie's name and Jimmy's name. More hands touched him and took him from Decker. Uncle Cully was there, anxiously gazing into his face. The world telescoped back into its proper place. Jimmy blinked.

Lassie leaned against his knees. Lyle Griffen, who was from South Dakota, held the reins of Geometry.

"What happened?" Jimmy asked, a little dizzy from all the excitement.

"Your horse saw a snake," said Uncle Cully. "She stopped so fast that she threw you. Then Lassie sailed in and pushed you out of the way. I'm not sure who was more scared, your horse or the snake."

"Did Lassie get bit?" Jimmy caught his breath. Sarah was kneeling and running her hands over the collie. Behind Sarah and Lassie, the students stood, each holding the reins of a riderless horse. The two pack mules stood motionless behind the crowd, not seeming to have even noticed what had just occurred.

Decker, his back to them, heaved rocks at nearby bushes, trying to scare out the rattlesnake. Jimmy bent down on one knee to help Sarah search Lassie's deep fur carefully with their fingers.

"It's hard to see a snake bite," said Karina. "Usually they get dogs on their noses."

Lassie's nose was unblemished. She didn't act sick. Snake poison usually hit the system fast, especially in smaller animals.

Fifteen minutes crept by and Lassie still acted normal.

"I think its safe to say she's okay," said Uncle Cully.

"Thank God," said Sarah.

Jimmy couldn't have agreed more. In fact, God had played a big part in the past few minutes of his life. *God is always there for me,* Jimmy thought. *Even if I don't have time to ask for help.*

A few minutes later Decker yelled and held up a limp snake body. "The dog bit the snake's head clean off."

"Lassie," said Jimmy, but he was unable to finish. He just put his arms around her neck, and she leaned into him for a long moment.

Decker deftly sliced off the rattles. Jimmy turned toward his horse, feeling queasy. Whether it was from the close call or the snake's dead body, he wasn't sure.

"You fell off this close to the snake," said Sarah, holding her hands less than a foot apart. "I could see it. Lassie jumped at you and rolled you away. Then she turned back to the snake." Sarah was quiet a moment, then said, "I guess that's when she killed it. She was so fast."

Thank You, God, for Lassie, was all Jimmy could think.

Decker swung the tailless, headless snake body around like a rope and let go, flinging it far from them.

"Ready to go on?" asked Uncle Cully.

Jimmy's arm ached, but it wasn't broken. Gingerly he touched his eyebrow. A lump the size of a marble throbbed painfully. He'd live. Jimmy was glad his uncle didn't fuss over him.

Thanks to Lassie he wasn't snake bitten. Having Lassie by your side was like having an extra guardian angel. Jimmy stroked Lassie's fur again and said, "I'm okay," to Uncle Cully. He took Geometry from Lyle, a geeky-looking white guy, thin with a big Adam's apple.

"Well, Geometry," he said to his mare. She turned her neck to look at him. "Could you warn me next time before slamming on the brakes?" The little mare blew gently onto the bruise over his eye. "I'll take that as a 'sorry,' " he said, checking the saddle cinch. He tightened it a notch, then swung up. His upper left arm was sore. He guessed he'd have a good bruise there tomorrow.

Finally the group rode off. Class seemed to be over for now and the students joked and talked. The notch in the mountain moved farther to his left, but Jimmy didn't say anything more about it.

As they rode on, Connor told him, "You've got yourself a nice looking black eye."

Jimmy touched his left eye. "I do?"

Connor nodded, still grinning. "I stopped counting the times I got shiners."

"How come you got so many black eyes?" asked Jimmy. He wondered if Connor used to be in a gang or something. Then he felt stupid for assuming that because he was black he had been in a gang.

Connor shrugged. "I just roughhoused a lot. Played street

hockey in the summer, ice hockey the winters. Ate a few pucks."

Jimmy laughed, thinking of Connor gnawing on a puck. Uncle Cully rode up beside Jimmy. "Still feeling okay?" he asked, then looked at him and whistled. "Nice bruise."

"Put a bag over your face, Jimmy," called Sarah. She was riding with Karina and Petra, who occasionally sent soap bubbles dancing. The two older girls smiled as Sarah giggled. They seemed to indicate that they knew what a pain younger sisters could be.

Girls! Jimmy just rolled his eyes then winced. He touched the lump over his eyebrow. "It could be a lot worse," he said, thinking of Lassie knocking him out of the way of the snake. She reacted so fast. He hadn't a clue what was going on. People so often said animals weren't smart, but both Lassie and Geometry had sensed the snake before any of the supposedly smarter humans, and they had avoided it.

Lassie trotted freely beside Geometry, not in the least bit sick, and Jimmy finally felt complete assurance that she hadn't been bitten by the snake. He thanked God again for keeping his dog well.

"We should be at the first ruins in another twenty minutes or so," said Uncle Cully. "Good thing. My rear is wishing for a soft chair."

Jimmy realized he'd been focusing on his aching bruises

instead of his sore leg muscles. Riding a horse looked so easy. You just sat there, right? Unless your horse tossed you! But riding used muscles that Jimmy usually didn't use, even with all the exercise he got running two miles a day.

As they approached a small butte several hundred feet high, Jimmy recognized it from Uncle Cully's description. The stony slab was hunched like a giant kid's slide.

"Is this Solitario Butte?" asked Sarah.

"It is," said Uncle Cully.

Karina corrected her pronunciation. "Sol-LE-tario." She rolled her r's effortlessly.

Sarah repeated the word, sounding a little better. Jimmy tried to roll his r's under his breath, too, but he sounded like a motor boat with engine trouble.

They rode part way around Solitario Butte. Flat land spread out around the butte for more than a mile in every direction. The jutting stone was solitary.

Uncle Cully halted his horse, the students and their horses crowding beside him. "Here it is," he called proudly as if he had helped create it.

The students and Sarah gasped and exclaimed.

Jimmy stared and couldn't see any ruins. Did the fall really rattle his brains, or what?

The Crack in the Wall

Jimmy stared longer at the rock slab, but still didn't see anything except rock. Maybe it was like those optical illusion books. You had to really stare at them before the colors and lines changed into pictures.

Lassie paused beside him, a tangle of burrs in her fur. He slid off Geometry, looping the reins on his arm, and picked the burrs out of Lassie's fur.

"Just between you and me," he said to her, "I don't think there's much to see." He knew Uncle Cully got excited over little bits of what seemed liked nothing to most people. But the funny thing was, Jimmy had seen photos of Anasazi ruins. They were cities built into the cliffs. Really cool. He wanted to see those. Not just scraps of rock.

Everyone had dismounted and was tending their horses. Grandpa had given instructions on how to unsaddle the horses and how to tie their legs together so they would stay nearby. "That's what it means to hobble the horses," he said.

Jimmy unknotted the cinch and pulled off the heavy

western saddle and the turquoise and red saddle blanket. Geometry's back was wet under the saddle. Carefully he wound the leather hobbles around the horse's front ankles, called fetlocks, and buckled them on. He took off the bridle. All the horses wore halters under their bridles. He left the halter on for now. At night he'd take it off to be safe. A horse could get hung up on a branch or fence and get strangled if the straps got caught.

"Go have some lunch, if you can find anything," said Jimmy. Back home in Iowa, the land would be green and lush with crops and pastures. Here, brown tufts of grass poked up among rocks and around a weird-looking cactus. The only green he saw was the cactus. Not very appetizing. But Geometry walked off, taking short strides because of the hobbles, and tore eagerly at the tufts of grass.

Whatever, thought Jimmy.

Decker was busy making lunch and fussed with one of the mule's packs.

Uncle Cully and his students, along with Sarah, had walked up to the edge of the butte. "Hey, Jim, going to join us some time?" Uncle Cully hollered.

Jimmy jumped up, and he and Lassie joined the others at the butte's edge. Ten feet up, an overhang bulged out. When he stepped into the shadows and looked up, his jaw dropped.

"What?" asked Sarah, her hands on her hips, her hair

33

whipping around her shoulders in the gusty wind, looking as if she belonged in the New Mexican landscape.

"There's a building in there," Jimmy said in awe. It was like an optical illusion. Look fast and it's a rock formation. Look again and it's a building.

"No kidding," said Sarah sarcastically. "What did you think we were looking at?"

The practical Anasazi had used the existing overhang as part of the wall and roof of the house. The door was a neat upside down T. A couple students were stepping inside.

Jimmy ran his hands over the stonework wall. "Incredible," he said. "Dad and I built a stone and mortar wall at church and—"

"We know," intoned Sarah. "It was one of the hardest things you have ever done."

Jimmy turned red as Uncle Cully and three of the students outside the ruins laughed. Karina was one of them, and he felt especially embarrassed. Sarah was such a brat. He glowered at her.

Lassie barked and ran to Sarah. She pawed at her, then ran back to Jimmy and whined.

"The counselor dog is at work," observed Uncle Cully. He explained to his students about Lassie and her peace-making mission. "She hates when anyone in my brother's family argues," said Uncle Cully.

"Well, don't invite her to my mother's village," said Karina.

"Lassie would go crazy trying to make peace with us!"

They laughed and Lassie relaxed her peace council.

Uncle Cully gathered up his students and began talking about the Anasazi, how the people had been there a thousand years ago and had probably come across the ice and land bridge between Asia and Alaska.

I wonder if the Anasazi ever heard of Jesus, thought Jimmy. *Were there any missionaries then? Naw, probably not.*

Jimmy waited until Uncle Cully and the students left the first small room. Sunshine angled in from the missing wall on one side. If the five foot tall room had all its walls, only the door would allow light in. *What a funny place,* he thought.

Uncle Cully said it was probably a storage area, for corn and other food. The stone floor was sandy. He scuffed his boots. Lassie's nails clicked on the stone under the sand, and she nudged Jimmy's hand with her nose.

"Hungry?" he asked her. He turned to go when his boots kicked some small stones. They rolled into the wall with clicks, bounced back out, and stopped in the path of sunlight.

They glittered. *Gold,* he thought jokingly to himself and reached down to pick them up. There were three stones, with eight sides each. Tiny beads were inlaid in different patterns on each side.

Like dice, he thought, turning each stone. For a game maybe?

The patterns didn't make much sense to him. It didn't look as if each bead represented numbers, like regular dice. There were too many beads to even count. Some beads were in squiggly lines, dashes, and angles.

He doubted whether they were Anasazi relics. The ruins were too picked over for that. Maybe another tribe, like the Navajo had left them. He'd have to ask Karina. He perked up. A good reason to talk to her.

Of course, with his luck the stones were probably made in Taiwan.

Jimmy stepped out of the ruin. Lassie was sniffing at a narrow crack in the main section of the butte.

Uncle Cully and the students had gone by it, seemingly not noticing it. He'd investigate. Who knew? Maybe it was a doorway into another ruin or some secret room. He'd check it out. Maybe he'd actually discover something that would put him in the annuls of history!

A Surprise from the Cave

The opening rose about seven feet high, as if a tall, narrow giant yawned. Lassie whined and scratched at the stone. At the base it was about the width of Jimmy's shoulders, so he began to push inside. It was dark.

Duh. Of course it was dark in caves. He pulled out his pen flashlight that had been tucked in his jeans pocket. The tiny beam shot over the stone. Jimmy stepped in sideways, careful not to jar his sore arm.

He was surprised. Uncle Cully hadn't said anything about the crack. Maybe it was another storage room, although this couldn't be man-made. He backed out and almost called to his uncle. But what if it were nothing but just that, a crack in the stone? Or worse, what if it were the Anasazi version of a bathroom? They'd all laugh. He'd had enough laughter at his expense today.

An odd musky smell drifted around him. It was familiar, but he couldn't place it.

Lassie whined again from the entrance.

"It's okay, girl," he called back. "I don't think this goes very far."

He walked four strides, then the stone narrowed too much to stand. He knelt and wriggled forward on his knees until the stone squeezed him to a stop. His light beam was narrow and only the size of a penny. But carefully, like a good archaeologist's helper, he swung the little light up and down the walls. Red and brown stone walls without any drawings or etchings flashed in and out of sight. He was glad he hadn't called Uncle Cully after all.

He couldn't turn around, so he shrugged back on his knees when a faint scratching stopped him. The noise was in front of him, not behind him where Lassie stood. She whined again.

Do snakes hide in caves? he thought suddenly. He sent the beam across the floor as far back as it would reach. Something moved just beyond the light. A shudder ran down his spine. He crawl backward fast and stood when the stone allowed. As he stood, he realized what the scent was.

Two beady eyes gleamed in the narrow beam. Then the eyes vanished and a black and white striped tail flipped in the light.

Jimmy yelled and shot out backward, crashing into Lassie who yelped. They sprawled over the edge of the stone and into the dirt and bushes.

38

Uncle Cully and the students ran toward him, fear on their faces.

Jimmy sprang up. "Run, run!" he shouted as the foul smell burst out of the crack in the wall.

Lassie barked fiercely as the skunk popped out, forelegs stiff, threatening. Then the striped creature turned around again.

Even though Jimmy's back was to the skunk, both his eyes watered. Girls and guys screamed.

They all ran from the butte, shrieking. The nearby horses spooked, and broke into jerking trots away from the stinking, running people.

Jimmy didn't stop until he was at Decker's small cook fire, ringed with stones. He looked back. The skunk was gone, but its presence lingered. So much for discovering anything that would place him in the annuls of history!

Decker and Sarah were laughing. Sarah, her journal in her hand, had tears running down her face.

The wind shifted. Sarah quit laughing and jumped up. "Pwee-yeeew!" she hollered and backed away.

Decker said, "That skunk's got a good aim."

Connor started laughing again. He sniffed his arms and hands. "Is it me or you all who stink?"

Lassie pawed at her nose, whining.

Jimmy put his arm around his collie. "The skunk didn't get you in your eyes, did it, girl?" Lassie's eyes weren't red or irritated, so he figured she must have turned in time. She kept shaking her fur as if trying to shake off the scent.

"Who was closest when she ripped?" asked Michael. "Was it you Lyle? You're not sleeping in my tent."

Lyle was holding his nose. "I think Petra was the closest."

Petra was raking off leaves of the sage bush and rubbing them on her arms and jeans. "Maybe this will help," she said. Even the pungent sage scent remained buried in the skunk smell though.

"I think we're doomed," said Michael.

"I'm sure not sleeping in a tent with any of you," declared Sarah.

"Who set the skunk off in the first place?" asked Uncle Cully.

Everyone looked at Jimmy. "Sorry," he choked, wishing he could fall off the edge of the earth. "There was this crack in the wall. I thought it was a cave with drawings, or maybe an Anasazi bathroom."

That set the college students off laughing. Uncle Cully clapped Jimmy's good shoulder. "That's the spirit, Jim. Never leave a rock or stone unturned."

Decker made chili and corn bread for lunch. Jimmy dug around in his pack for his bowl. He wondered if he ought to change his clothes, but he only had one other set of clothes. Everyone had saddlebags for their stuff, and that was it. Not much room for extras. If he changed now he'd have to wear those clothes for another three days. Oh well. The scent was probably in his hair anyway, and changing clothes wouldn't help.

The students and Uncle Cully sat down around the cook fire with bowls of chili and wedges of corn bread. Jimmy sat near them.

Michael said, "Why does my chili taste like skunk?"

"Maybe we'll get used to the smell," suggested Karina.

Jimmy grinned. "Maybe we'll even learn to like it. It could be a new fashion statement."

"Saying what? Don't come near me?"

"It could protect you from muggers," suggested Jimmy.

"Maybe you're on to something," she said and winked.

His face flushed under her attention, then he busied himself eating.

He sure was having trouble staying out of trouble. How was he supposed to know a skunk was in the crack?

He could almost hear Dad's preaching voice in his ear, "Skunk? I'd say that smell is a lot like sin. You get tangled up in it, and it stays for a long, miserable time."

Even when you stumble onto to it by accident?

"That's how sin works."

Jimmy smiled. He'd have to tell Dad. He'd like the analogy.

41

Tower in the Desert

After lunch they mounted up and rode onto the next site. Then they traveled toward Little Lizard Canyon.

"We'll camp just outside the canyon," Uncle Cully said. "There are some pictographs on the rocks we can examine. That will be our base camp. Then in the morning we can go on into the canyon."

As Jimmy approached Geometry, the mare curled her nostrils as if she didn't like Jimmy's smell. "Sorry," Jimmy told her. "I don't like it either."

Fortunately a brisk wind came along and pushed a lot of the smell away into the desert. Or maybe he was just getting used to it.

They rode for another three hours, crossing sand and more sand and two sets of rocky hills. The Cebolleta Mountains grew closer and climbed the sky in pale green. The sun rode on their peaks. The notch was out of sight. Jimmy tried not to think about that.

A steep, narrow shaft of black rock reared up. Uncle

Cully pulled up his horse and said, "Let's climb it quick. I want you all to see something. Then we have to hurry on to the canyon."

They left Decker with the horses and mules. Then the nine of them, including Lassie, climbed a steep, narrow butte that jutted up as if some creature were under the earth pushing it out. That idea made Jimmy's skin creep, so instead he thought of a gentle giant creating a sand castle. That was a better image.

The climb was steep. Jimmy panted as the skinny path wound around the stone higher and higher. *Funny what the wind and water erosion did,* he thought. It was as if steps were carved into the stone. Lassie scrambled up the stone stairs after him, her tongue hanging to her chest.

Jimmy, Lassie, and Karina reached the top first. The winds snapped by like invisible bullet trains.

Karina smiled at him. "Do you run?" she asked.

He nodded and said a little breathlessly, "Do you?"

She nodded. "I want to run the Boston Marathon next year after I graduate."

"Cool," he said. "The farthest I've run has been seven miles."

"That's good," she said. "I'm still working up to twenty-six miles—the distance of a marathon. Some of my people run the ancient trails and cover a hundred miles in a day."

"No way!" exclaimed Jimmy. "A hundred miles!"

Her dark eyes sparkled. "It's true. Maybe some day you will visit our village and run with the men."

"I'd like that," he said humbly. He would like that.

The others straggled up after them.

Jimmy walked around the top of the butte, a mini-mesa about the size of a hockey rink. In middle was a crumbling tower. What was left of it rose at least two stories. The roof had collapsed, and one side had crumpled as if something had rammed it.

Uncle Cully, panting and wiping sweat from his forehead, put a hand on the tower stone wall. "What do you think this is?" He pointed a finger at Karina. "You be quiet."

She smiled and moved away to the edge.

"It looks like a tower," offered Lyle.

"Good," said Uncle Cully. "What was it used for?"

"A lookout," suggested Connor.

"Defense?" asked Petra. "Like to watch for the enemy?"

"Some think that. Look around you," said Uncle Cully. "See anything unusual?"

The five students walked around the edge of the butte top. Jimmy and Lassie trailed after them. Sarah sat down on a stone and lifted handfuls of black, white, and red sand. The wind snatched the smaller, lighter pieces and carried them away.

As Petra looked, she blew bubbles that shot away on the wind and shattered on stones.

Jimmy stood at the edge of the mesa and searched the landscape. The sun glared low in the sky. Long shadows draped over the sands.

Karina walked past Jimmy and said causally, "Remember those long miles running."

Huh?

"No hints," warned Uncle Cully. Karina smiled and walked on.

A big black bird flew past, croaking, its clever head turned, looking at them. Jimmy searched the desert. Suddenly he saw straight lines radiating out from the butte. Or was it an illusion from the shadows? Or just an idea that Karina planted in his head?

Jimmy circled the edge of the butte again. Sure enough, faint lines, maybe only as wide as a sidewalk, shot directly out. They were perfectly straight, not meandering things like the horse trail they'd been riding.

He counted at least five paths leading away from the butte. They were all perfectly straight.

"Uncle Cully," he said and swallowed, hoping there wasn't a skunk somewhere in his idea. "There are roads in the desert."

His uncle smiled as the students stared at Jimmy dumbfounded. Karina turned to him with a triumphant grin.

"Roads? Where?" asked Lyle. Jimmy pointed them out and the others crowded around.

"So there are roads," said Uncle Cully. "Then what is this structure?" He patted the tower again.

"A signaling device?" said Petra, and she blew a long line of soap bubbles. "Maybe smoke during the day and a fire at night."

"Bingo," said Uncle Cully.

"I still don't see the roads," said Michael. Karina and Jimmy pointed out the long, lean paths, so faint, worn, and old, but visible in the slanting sunlight.

"The Anasazi didn't have animals to ride or even carts to use, because they didn't have the wheel. Their roads were footpaths," said Uncle Cully. "We've seen many of them through recent aerial photography and thermo-imaging. More than a 1000 miles of roads in the desert are documented. But the roads were more extensive than that. They had major trade routes, from Mexico to California and even up north as far as Canada."

"That's incredible," said Connor.

"It is," said Uncle Cully. "The Anasazi had great cultural centers, religious centers, and economic centers."

Karina added quietly, "My grandmother has a necklace that has been in our clan for years and years. It's made out of abalone shell from California."

"If they were signaling, what were they saying?" asked Michael.

Sarah piped up. "Birthdays and stuff?"

"That could be," said Uncle Cully. "Maybe letting others know a shipment had come in. Perhaps calling the righteous for religious ceremonies."

"Maybe they had certain colors of smoke for certain events," said Jimmy.

They poked around a little more, then headed back down the butte. Jimmy realized the pathway of steps wasn't from erosion, but had been deliberately cut into the stone. He burst out, "They must have worked hard. All these buildings and roads."

"They were farmers and had irrigation systems," added Uncle Cully.

"I thought cavemen types were kind of stupid," said Sarah. "That's what people always say anyhow."

"I think the opposite," said Uncle Cully. "Ancient man was smart, clever. The things they accomplished are incredible."

"Their gene pool was better," said Karina. "They were that much closer to the first people."

"Adam and Eve," breathed Sarah. "Wow."

Karina smiled at her. "Or something like them."

Wow was right. Part way down the path, Jimmy looked back up once more. The raven sat on top of the tower, the wind ruffling his feathers, looking like the very first bird.

7

Where Are the Hot Springs?

They jostled on toward Little Lizard Canyon. As the sun dipped below the mountaintops, everything plunged into twilight. Geometry didn't stumble, but just in case Jimmy kept a tight hold onto the saddle horn. So what if the others thought he was a sissy? He didn't want to have the ground catch him a second time.

Jimmy squinted at the line of mountains, but it was too dark to see the notch. He wanted to like Decker, to trust him, but he felt uneasy around the man.

A sudden flood of dark forms winged overhead. High pitched squeaking bounced through the skies. Bats. *Cool,* thought Jimmy. *Where are the caves?* he wondered. He stared all around him, but the shadows had grown too long and deep to distinguish much. In the east, a red glow over the tops of the Sangre de Cristo Mountains promised to light the night once the lopsided moon rose.

Funny how it's always a full moon on Easter, thought

Jimmy. Easter was just five days away. Was it really a full moon when Christ rose from the grave?

Something jetted past, and in a nasal voice called: beeerp!

Jimmy jumped, and Decker chuckled from beside him, the tattoos of his horse and two mules keeping rhythm with Jimmy's pounding heart.

"Just a nighthawk," said Decker. "Ever seen one before?"

"I don't think so," said Jimmy.

"Little bird, like a roan horse, gray, white, black, and brown. They eat insects, like bats do."

They rode on, the desert and mountains unfurling endlessly. *If I were in a wagon train,* thought Jimmy, *I'd be scared, never knowing when the land would end.*

"Are we close to the canyon?" Jimmy asked.

"Sure are," said Decker. "If it were a snake, it would have bit you by now."

Jimmy swallowed hard, his snake episode still quite clear in his brain. Decker spurred his ugly horse past and didn't seem to think twice about his words being frightening. Or maybe he meant them to be mean.

Jimmy sighed. Being a pastor's kid, you learned there were all kinds of people.

Up ahead Uncle Cully and Decker talked about campsites and water availability.

"Look," said Sarah suddenly. Jimmy turned. His sister

and her horse shone in the rush of molten silver from the moon scaling the mountains. The gold of Sarah's hair and Calculus' fur turned into cool sterling.

"Whoa, Calculus," said Sarah. Jimmy stopped Geometry beside her.

"You want to drink the stuff or something," said Sarah, cupping her hand in the moonlight. Jimmy turned his face up to the light.

Half the moon had risen above the jagged peaks; then the rest of the moon popped up, like a beach ball shooting out of the water.

Their horses were tired and glad to rest. They stood while Sarah and Jimmy watched. Lassie stood in the light, sharp muzzled as a coyote about to sing moon songs.

"Jimmy, Sarah, almost there," called Uncle Cully. "Stay together."

Reluctantly Jimmy and Sarah urged their horses on. Lassie silked beside them, her fur cold fire. *She is a creature of the night,* thought Jimmy, *fitting perfectly into the desert.* Uncle Cully had said that the Anasazi had dogs for pets. Could Lassie sense all the thousands, hundreds of thousands of dogs that had run this desert before her?

He shook himself. That was ridiculous. Only moon madness. He could tell however, that she heard something that interested her. Her ears pricked nearly upright and she gazed off into the distance, keeping time with them on the horses, but intensely listening.

Then he heard it, too. Sharp yaps and shrill howls mixed together with the silver of moon in a fine melody and harmony of the night.

Coyotes. It was impossible to tell how many. Their voices rose, fell, stilled, started up, quieted. When the moon had climbed higher, rising over all the mountains, Decker called, "We are here."

Stiffly, Jimmy swung off Geometry. If his horse were as sore as he was, they would both be in big trouble.

"Where are those mineral hot springs?" asked Karina. She stood beside her horse, stroking her neck. "I sure could use them."

"Best thing for saddle stiffness," said Decker.

"Lead me to it," said Connor.

Canyon walls yawned up, forbidding, dark, impenetrable even by the almost full moon's light. Jimmy unbuckled the headstall and pulled off Geometry's bridle. The horse immediately dropped his head to munch the tufts of grass.

"Tend the horses, then set up camp before any hot springs," said Uncle Cully. Everyone groaned as they slid off their horses, pulled saddles off, and hobbled them to graze the night away.

"There's water over here," said Karina. A narrow trickle of water tumbled out of the canyon.

"Funny," said Decker, "I thought the Little Lizard was dry. There's a spring part way into the canyon."

"That's right," said Karina suddenly. "There are a couple more springs, not the mineral hot ones, deeper in the canyon. My uncle told me."

"Maybe there have been rains recently?" suggested Uncle Cully.

Both Karina and Decker shook their heads. "No rain in weeks. Not since early February."

"God is kind," said Uncle Cully with a shrug. "Water nearby and I'm thankful."

Jimmy helped pitch the three tents. Then he dragged his saddlebags to the tent farthest from the cook fire. For the next hour they all settled themselves in camp. Jimmy and Connor dug two pits for toilets, well away from the stream. Jimmy laughed when Lyle dragged up some fallen branches to use as seats. "Might as well be comfortable," said Lyle. They screened the lavatory with a tarp.

Then they ate dinner. Jimmy and Sarah were in charge of dish washing. They stood at the small river's edge with a small tub with suds. First they let Lassie clean all the plates with her expert tongue.

"I say let's just put the plates back," Sarah said. "Lassie cleaned them real good." Jimmy just laughed and thought he wouldn't mind so much, but he had a feeling the others would.

Jimmy scrubbed the pots Decker had cooked in with sand, then together he and Sarah soaped up the dishes and silverware in a plastic bucket. Finally they rinsed everything with fresh water. Sarah dried it all with a towel. Jimmy held up a tin plate to the ever-present wind. "Dries faster this way," he said with a smile.

While they washed and air dried the dishes, Karina and Uncle Cully had re-saddled their horses and ridden up the canyon to check out the hot springs.

As Jimmy picked up the clean dishes, he stared at the moon's reflection in a small pool of water. Did an Anasazi kid stare into this river on a moon-filled night? Probably.

About a half hour later, Uncle Cully and Karina clattered back down the trail.

With moonlight dripping over her, Karina called out, "This isn't Little Lizard Canyon. There aren't any hot springs." As if on cue, Karina and her horse suddenly dropped as if an elevator went down.

Karina didn't make any sound, but her horse shrieked in a way that Jimmy would never forget.

A Horse Set Free

Everyone ran toward them.

But both Uncle Cully and Karina were shouting, "Stay back! Stay back! Quicksand!"

Triangle had sunk up to her shoulders. She tried to plunge, her eyes bulging, showing white all the way around the irises, but she could scarcely shift her bulk. The sand held her tighter than any rope lariat. In frustration, the mare banged her head against the ground.

"No, no!" cried Karina. She lay on her belly to distribute her weight and touched the mare's muzzle. "Hold still, girl."

Lassie light-footed around to Triangle's head and whined softly. The mare banged her head again.

Lassie stood on the edge of solid ground, whining quietly. She sought to make eye contact with Triangle who was tossing her mane and snorting, but her glassy gaze kept returning to the collie's earnest eyes.

"Like herding sheep. She's making the horse pay attention to her," murmured Petra. "Smart dog."

Jimmy wondered how Petra, a girl from Newark, New Jersey, knew about dogs and sheep.

But that was what Lassie was trying to do. Gain Triangle's gaze and hypnotize the mare to calm her.

"Quiet," said Jimmy. "Please. Lassie is calming Triangle down." Everyone stopped talking and silently watched Lassie work.

The mare stopped banging her head. Lassie crouched low, whining, staring intently into the mare's face. Triangle rolled her eyes but gazed back at the dog.

By now the quicksand was oozing over Triangle's back.

"Someone saddle another horse," commanded Decker. Connor hurried off into the darkness. Decker continued quietly, "We'll get a rope on the mare's neck and pull her out."

Everyone automatically obeyed Decker. "Stay with your dog," Decker told Jimmy. "Don't let her get in the quicksand, though I don't think she will. She's smart."

Jimmy knelt beside his dog. She didn't take her eyes off Triangle who was staring back at her, but her tail wagged a moment, acknowledging him. Jimmy held himself very still, not wanting to break the spell upon the mare.

For it were as if a spell had been lain. Triangle stared into the dog's eyes. The dark eyes quit rolling, and her snorting stopped.

Connor came back with a saddled horse.

Quickly Decker shook out the loop and dropped it over

Triangle's neck. He then turned the rope a couple times around Uncle Cully's saddle horn. "Keep it taut. Back your horse up slowly," he said.

When the rope tightened, Triangle broke the gaze, struggled again, trying to plunge. Lassie whined, and when the mare returned her gaze to the dog, she stayed quieted. White flecks of sweat spotted her neck.

"Nothing a horse hates more," muttered Decker as he signaled Uncle Cully to back his horse again, "being down and helpless."

Is that how we all are, horses and humans? wondered Jimmy. Terrified to be down in the dark, helpless. Jesus was the One who pulled us out.

Decker secured a second rope to the horse Connor had brought up. He tied the other end of the rope around a fallen branch he'd picked up. "Hold this," said Decker passing the rope end to Michael. Then carefully Decker poked his branch about where Triangle's tail should be. As he pushed the branch through the heavy sand, it cracked. Decker swore, found another branch, and tried again. Finally he managed to loop the branch under Triangle's tailbone and tie the rope to her tail.

"I'm losing her," said Uncle Cully quietly. His horse was straining, the rope tight from the saddle horn to the mare's neck, but was being dragged inch by inch toward the quicksand that wasn't satisfied with just one victim.

Triangle's eyes were half-closed, barely focusing on Lassie. *Can horses faint?* wondered Jimmy. Probably, especially with a rope closing off her windpipe.

Decker moved fast, his hand on the taut rope, lightly running to his horse and swinging up.

"Stand clear," Decker told Jimmy who backed up and wondered if he should call off Lassie. She was still gazing into the downed horse's eyes. But he decided that so far, Lassie had known what she was doing, and he figured she still did. So he let her be.

"On the count of three," Decker told Uncle Cully. Uncle Cully turned his horse around so it could pull forward instead of backing up. All the students and Sarah stood near, worried expressions on their faces. Petra looked as if she were holding her breath.

When Decker said the word *three,* both riders kicked their horses who plunged forward. Triangle started to squeal, then the rope cut her voice in half.

Her muddy tail stuck straight up in the rope's grip. The twin ropes slowly hauled her up like a great, muddy treasure being recovered. Lassie jumped back as the mare thrashed, a foreleg lashing free. Both men yelled at their horses who pulled harder.

Jimmy held his breath.

Slowly the sand released the mare, body part by body part—shoulders, hips, rump, back legs, knees. The sand gurgled and made awful sucking noises like a great beast puking up the mare.

The two horses gave a final burst of speed, and Triangle completely slid out of the quicksand like a newborn foal. Her forelegs stretched out in front of her as she gasped for air on her belly, Her body was dark with wet sand.

"Whoa," commanded Decker. His horse and Uncle Cully's stopped, heads tossing. The two ropes slackened. Before anyone could move, Karina and Lassie swooped beside Triangle. Karina crooned and wiped at the mud while Lassie licked clean the mare's nostrils, eyes, and ears.

Triangle lay unmoving on the ground, eyes open, but glazed.

"She's in shock," said Decker. "Let her be. She'll come around." He slipped the neck and tail ropes off her. With Connor's help, they unsaddled her, yanking the cinch out from under her belly.

That seemed to rouse the mare. She thrust her forelegs forward, rocked her body, then rose on shaking legs.

Karina threw her arms around the mare's neck. Jimmy ran to Triangle's hip, and with both hands helped steady her. Lassie barked while the rest of the students and Uncle Cully cheered as the moonlight poured down, flooding the area with its silver glow.

Scorpions for Breakfast

After settling Triangle, the other horses, and themselves, all anyone wanted to do was collapse into sleeping bags.

"Not that we saw any mineral springs anyway," Karina had said loudly from her tent.

The next morning they resumed the topic.

Karina and Decker went at it rather strongly. "So you're telling me I didn't take you to Little Lizard Canyon?" Decker demanded.

Karina leaned over Triangle's front knee, applying a poultice made from canyon plants. The poultice would help draw out the soreness and help heal the leg. When she straightened up, she stared at Decker and said, "Look, I'm not accusing you of anything. I'm just stating the facts. This is not Little Lizard Canyon."

Jimmy came out of his tent, Lassie at his heels.

"How's Triangle doing?" he asked in a bright voice, hating the angry tones.

Uncle Cully must have felt the same, for he fed more

sticks into the fire and said, "Isn't this about ready for cooking? I'm starved."

Decker stomped back to the fire.

Whether it is the right canyon or not, thought Jimmy, *it looks exciting.* In the morning light, he could see that the canyon walls rose north and west. The red and tan rocks were sharply craggy. The stream was approximately three feet across, but the sand extending out from it was more than ten feet on both sides.

The spot where Triangle had gone down looked like every other section of sand. Someone had stuck branches around the area to keep everyone out. But how did you know where the sand was dangerous?

"What tracks are all around our tents?" asked Sarah as she came back from her mini-interviews.

"Looks like kangaroo rat tracks," said Uncle Cully as he scraped dried mud from his boots with a stone.

"Rats!" said Sarah. "Ick!"

"Kangaroo rats are cute," Uncle Cully said. "They just hop around and collect seeds. They don't hurt anyone."

"Rats!" said Sarah again. "Ick."

Decker looked up from baking biscuits. "Those tracks aren't rats. They're scorpion."

"Scorpion!" exclaimed everyone within earshot.

Decker nodded. "Sure thing. They crawl out just before dawn looking for food."

"My skin is itching," said Petra. "I think one's crawling on me." She whacked at her jeans and jumped around.

"I don't believe that," said Sarah. "How could there be fifty million scorpion tracks? They're everywhere."

Jimmy crouched down to study the tracks. "Don't scorpions have six legs and two claws? Just a few scorpions would make a lot of tracks."

Lyle grimaced. "I'm not sure that makes me feel better."

Sarah called to Karina. She seemed to be the local expert, next to Decker.

"What tracks are these?" asked Sarah pointing around her.

Karina barely looked up from Triangle's leg. "Scorpion."

Petra and Lyle groaned.

"I'm not sleeping on the ground again!" said Sarah. She stood accusingly over Uncle Cully who was still cleaning his boots. "You didn't tell us scorpions would be here."

Uncle Cully smiled sweetly up at her. "You didn't ask me."

"Uncle Cully!" She glared at him as if he personally loaded the desert with scorpions.

Lassie whined and pawed at Sarah, trying to comfort her.

"Just keep your tent zipped up tight," Decker called. "Scorpions don't want to tangle with humans."

"I'm sleeping on my horse tonight," Sarah said.

Sarah popped back into the girls' tent, muttering about desert monsters. Uncle Cully and Jimmy and Lassie had shared the second tent with Lyle; Connor and Michael Doh, the Vietnamese guy from southern California, were in the third tent. Decker claimed he slept better outside, even though the guys had teased him about not liking their new cologne, Ode de Skunk.

Finally as everyone ate, Jimmy quietly asked Uncle Cully, "So is this the right canyon or what?"

Uncle Cully set down his tin cup of coffee. "I've been looking at the map," he said. "Something I should have done yesterday. Karina appears to be right as far as I can tell."

Then Jimmy told Uncle Cully what Grandpa had said about keeping the notch straight in front of them, and about the compass bearings he had taken. After looking over the map, they found the notch. Sure enough, Little Lizard Canyon was in direct line with it. Also the compass bearings Jimmy took matched up to the notch.

"So where are we?" asked Jimmy.

"Close to Little Lizard Canyon," Uncle Cully replied.

They hunched over the map some more. Decker kept glancing at them, and Jimmy had a sick feeling in his stomach. Decker hadn't listened to him yesterday and now acted as if Karina were just causing trouble. What would Decker say to Uncle Cully and the map?

"I think we're here," said Uncle Cully, pointing at a canyon labeled Echo Cliffs. "See, the stream, Echo Wash, is more or less year 'round. I think this is the trail we were on yesterday."

Uncle Cully sighed. He put his hand on Jimmy's shoulder and said, "Do me a favor?"

"Sure." Jimmy would do anything for his uncle.

"Say a prayer, because this might be sticky."

"Don't worry, Uncle Cully," Jimmy said. "God knows where we are, and He can help us get through this okay."

"I wish I had your faith, Jim." Uncle Cully acted concerned. "I guess I'm still learning. I must be the oldest babe in Christ that ever lived," he said, referring to his conversion last summer.

"Dad says it doesn't matter when we start," Jimmy said, "as long as we're committed."

"I don't know how that brother of mine got so smart," Cully said. "He must be living right."

"Well, he gets a lot of help," Jimmy said, pointing his finger toward the sky. "And, of course, his wonderful family, mainly his extraordinary son, helps a lot and . . ."

"Never mind, I get the picture," Uncle Cully added with a smile. "You pray and I'll get everyone rounded up."

Jimmy did pray while Uncle Cully gathered everyone together, including Decker.

"Here's the scoop," said Uncle Cully. He laid the map on the ground and put a rock on each edge. "Here is Little Lizard Canyon. But this is where we are."

Everyone except Sarah and Jimmy crowded around, murmuring. Sarah sat with Lassie, combing the collie's long tangled fur, with a frown on her face.

"That just can't be," exclaimed Decker. "I know this country."

"Ten miles," said Lyle. "We're off by a good ten miles."

"Triangle isn't going anywhere," said Karina, flatly. "Her knee is blown. If she walks on it, as if we could even get her to move, I'm afraid she'll permanently damage it."

"We only have three days," said Connor. "If we tear down this camp and set up another, we'll lose practically half a day, maybe more."

Jimmy sat with his chin on his knees, praying that Decker wouldn't cause trouble. He didn't think Decker had done this on purpose. His memory was just shot.

Uncle Cully took Decker aside. They stood by the river, talking and pointing. Jimmy couldn't hear their words, just the rise and fall of their voices.

Karina sat with her knees drawn up. She hadn't said anything, and her silence shook Jimmy. A stricken expression took hold of her.

He was on his feet and at her side before he realized he'd even moved. "What's wrong?" he asked.

"We're at Echo Cliffs? I can't believe it. We're in big trouble," she said.

The Story of Echo Cliffs

Everyone stared at Karina. Jimmy wanted to take her arm, but he was afraid to. She clenched her fists, stood and stopped, looking scared.

"You did this on purpose, didn't you, Decker?" Karina demanded. "Why?"

Jimmy backed away, but Lassie didn't. The big collie had risen at Karina's first cries. Now she whined and pawed at Karina's leg. Karina pushed past the collie and headed for Decker by the fire. Uncle Cully was on his feet moving toward Karina.

"Now look here," said Decker, his hands on his hips. "This is a big mistake. I've just mixed up my canyons. It's easy to do. They all look alike. You know that." He put his hands out pleadingly, but Karina still advanced on him as if she were going to punch his face.

Lassie quickly slipped between the two of them. When Karina didn't stop, the collie jumped up, her paws on Karina's chest, halting the girl.

"We need to talk this out," said Uncle Cully. "Karina, stop. Decker, come here." Decker had been heading for the river as if he were going to jump in and swim away.

Uncle Cully set them down on opposite sides of the map and motioned the rest of his students closer. Jimmy and Sarah sat on either side of Uncle Cully. Karina's cheeks were an angry flush of red and Decker's eyes were sullen.

Lassie sat beside Karina, whining and occasionally licking the girl's chin. Jimmy nervously put his hand in his jacket pocket and found the many-sided stones with inlaid beads. He played with them, easing his nervousness.

Uncle Cully smiled a little when Karina finally patted the collie.

"Thank you, Lassie," said Uncle Cully. "Every court in America should have a Lassie. Okay, let's just state the facts and leave our emotions out. We're ten miles or so from the canyon we planned on exploring. One of our horses is injured and is not to be used. Do you still want to move to Little Lizard Canyon or stay here at Echo Cliffs, which is where we think we are?"

"I say let's explore this canyon. Traces of the Anasazi people are everywhere. This will just make us look harder. It'll be fun," said Connor.

Petra tapped her soap bubble container. "Little Lizard Canyon had all those cool petroglyph etchings."

"Yes," said Uncle Cully. "But you have seen photos of

them. Perhaps we'll find new ones here."

Uncle Cully turned to Decker. "How long has it been since you were at Little Lizard Canyon?"

Decker pursed his lips. "Twenty years, maybe, when I was a hand over at Kellerman's cattle ranch."

Twenty years ago! Jimmy thought. That's when Jimmy realized Decker wasn't a bad guy, just another person who blew it. Dad was fond of saying that most people meant well but generally did the wrong thing for different reasons. "That's why we're supposed to forgive each other seventy times seven," Dad would tell Jimmy when he was mad at his best friends Blake and Katie, or bugged with his sister, Sarah.

"Twenty years was a long time ago," said Uncle Cully.

"I was sure I remembered it was this way," Decker said. He tapped his head. "I could see it so clear."

"Either way it's a gamble," said Lyle. "Personally, I don't relish getting back on a horse today. I'm majorly sore."

"How about the rest of you?" asked Uncle Cully. "Should we stay here?"

"You just don't understand," Karina burst out.

Decker stabbed at the sand with a stick as if he did understand and was sorry or mad or something. Jimmy couldn't figure out the guy.

"Karina, let's hear your side," Uncle Cully said.

Without glancing at Decker she said tightly, "Look, I

know you probably don't believe in old Indian stories, but there is a tale about this canyon." Karina stopped and stared up the canyon. The wind was cool over Jimmy's face.

"And?" Uncle Cully prompted her.

"And," Karina continued, "the story goes that it's called Echo Cliffs because you can hear your voice echo when you're in the canyon. But also it's said that whatever happens in this canyon will be repeated, echoed if you will, in the rest of the world."

"But if all we're doing is looking," said Uncle Cully, "how can that be bad?"

"Because," said Karina staring hard at Decker now, "the old stories tell of bad things that happen. Hardly anything good happens here."

No one said anything for a minute. Jimmy tried to figure out what she meant. If they found some old thing, like a bowl, that an Anasazi had made, then one of Karina's people would find an old bowl? That wasn't bad, was it? She must mean if something happened like a fight in the canyon, then a fight would break out in the Indian tribe? Wasn't that just superstition?

"Karina," said Uncle Cully, gently. "Do you really believe this tale?" His unspoken words were, "Or are you just being stubborn?" Jimmy knew his uncle's silent language, so like Dad's.

She bit her lip and glanced at Triangle grazing nearby, her

leg neatly bandaged. "Yes, I believe. Well, no, not exactly." Then she frowned, "I don't know. I just know this place is talked of in bad terms. It kind of makes me nervous."

Uncle Cully said gently, "Karina, you don't have to go into the canyon. There are other things you can do out here."

The other four students nodded their heads slowly.

Jimmy was surprised to see tears in Karina's eyes. But after a moment, she nodded and all the fire seemed to go out of her. She said, "It's okay, Dr. Harmon. I'll go in, too."

Uncle Cully turned to Decker again. "Did you know about this canyon? Echo Cliffs?"

Decker gave Karina a swift glance. "No, sir," he said. "Never heard the story before."

Karina gave a little snort.

"That's the truth, Miss," said Decker. "I'm sorry to have brought this on you all. I mean it."

Karina met Decker's gaze for a half second and gave him a quick nod.

"I reckon it's just an old Indian tale," said Petra. "That's cool. I can deal with it."

"So what about the rest of you?" asked Uncle Cully. "Do you want to do this canyon or try for Little Lizard?"

The other four murmured together, but quickly agreed that they wanted to stay.

Michael said, "I'd like to explore the canyon. Maybe

we'll find some new things. Especially if the canyon's been, you know, sacred."

"Not exactly sacred," said Karina. "More like the opposite of that."

"God is in the business of redemption," said Uncle Cully, briskly. "I think He can manage for us. How about you, Jim and Sarah?"

Sarah shrugged. "It's okay with me to stay, Uncle Cully."

Jimmy stroked Lassie's fur. "I don't mind staying either. If we did go to Little Lizard Canyon, what would we do about Triangle since she's not fit to travel?"

Uncle Cully gave a small shrug. "That's a problem. It may still be a problem when we return," he said. "It's something to think about."

Jimmy turned to Karina. "Will your relatives be upset if we go into the canyon?"

"Good question," murmured Uncle Cully.

Karina considered. She gazed up at the stone cliffs, her eyes dark and unreadable. Finally she said, "No, I think it will be all right after all. It is an old tale and more a superstition, I think. I can remember adults scaring us kids with it, like a ghost story."

"Agreed then?" asked Uncle Cully. Everyone nodded. "Then I want us all ready to move out in fifteen minutes."

The Ancient Orchard

Jimmy got his daypack. He made sure he had his essential items: small first aid kit, water purifying system, granola bars, matches, space blanket, lightweight tarp for emergency tent, Lassie's food, sunglasses, and compass. He carried Lassie's dog booties because some of the rocks were razor sharp, and if she stepped on one wrong, her paws could be sliced.

When he poked his head out of his tent, everyone else was still getting ready. Laughter came from one of the guys' tents. Decker was sorting through the unloaded mule packs.

Jimmy hoisted his pack and stood by the stream. Echo Cliffs gradually rose up higher and higher as the canyon walls leaned in closer. About an eighth of a mile down the canyon, its path turned, so the only way to see the canyon was to go in.

"Jimmy," said Sarah, her eyes serious. "What about the people who lived here."

"What about them?"

"Did they go to heaven?"

Jimmy knew what she saying. What about other cultures, like the Navajo, the Hopi and all the many other tribes here and throughout the world? Their ancient ways weren't centered around Jesus, so what happened to them?

He took a deep breath. "I think God calls everybody, and He knows who answers and who ignores Him, even if those people didn't grow up hearing about Him. I think Jesus can call those who are still living so they'll understand."

Jimmy watched Uncle Cully as he talked to the college students around their tents. Uncle Cully had given his life to Jesus after many years of hearing the Gospel over and over. Finally Uncle Cully accepted it. Was it harder or easier if you had never heard much about Jesus?

"So did the Anasazi go to heaven?" asked Sarah.

"I don't know how it works, but God is fair, unlike most people. The ones who love Him will be there in heaven."

She made a face. "That's not a very good answer."

He laughed. "Sorry. But you're just going to end up asking Dad when you get home anyway." He laughed inside, knowing his little sister was like a puppy chasing a ball. She'd never quit until she had her answers.

Jimmy wandered over to Karina, who was tending Triangle. Decker was nearby, sorting through packs. He would stay behind and tend camp and the horses. Karina had left a fresh poultice for him to put on Triangle's knee.

"What is this stuff, anyhow?" Decker complained. "It

stinks almost as bad as the skunk smell."

"Jimson weed," Karina grinned and said. "Nasty stuff, but it works."

Decker held his nose, then turned his back on them all as if they smelled. They probably did still reek of skunk, but Jimmy hadn't even noticed it today.

Lassie trotted down to the stream to drink. The shooting star flowers wobbled around her like butterflies. Jimmy pulled out his small camera and snapped a few photos.

Above the rocky cliffs the sky was a hard cobalt blue. Gray clouds rippled in the winds like running horses. Last night Uncle Cully and Karina hadn't been able to ride very far into the canyon; it was narrow, which was why they were hiking in now.

"Do you think Dad would mind if we went into the canyon? You know how he is about respecting others' beliefs," asked Sarah. Jimmy jumped. She had come up so quietly he hadn't heard her.

"I think if Uncle Cully says it's okay, then Dad would too," said Jimmy. "Karina thought it was going to be okay."

Sarah nodded. Lassie returned from the stream and leaned against her knees. "Besides, we have Lassie," said Sarah.

He laughed. "Between Lassie and Jesus, I think we're super safe."

Finally Uncle Cully rounded them up, and they began hiking along a faint trail into Echo Cliffs.

As they walked, Jimmy saw the scat of wild rabbits. Last night he'd again heard the coyotes singing. Lassie had also been awake, head raised, ears pricked, but she was quiet, not barking or howling in return. Jimmy wondered if she understood the language of the coyote. Was it a dialect of dog? Or a totally different language?

Some of the students strayed off the trail, scrambling up stony inclines, making stones tumble and dirt rattle down. Karina snapped pictures of stone piles, which Jimmy thought were kind of boring. One larger boulder had some brown and black paint drawings, but Uncle Cully and Karina agreed they were Navajo and not very old.

Petra blew soap bubbles. One landed on Lassie's ear and clung there, as if hitching a ride.

"Now look at the patina," said Uncle Cully.

"The what-a?" asked Sarah.

"Patina," repeated Michael. "It's like corrosion from rain water streaming down the cliffs."

They all stopped and looked up at the cliff rising hundreds of feet high. Streaks of brown and black, thousands of feet long, lined the canyon walls. Uncle Cully talked some more about layers of rocks and periods of time with weird names. Sarah sat on a rock and Jimmy wandered farther along the path with Lassie trailing him.

The narrow, dusty path led down to a clearing about thirty feet above the snaking stream. Just past the clearing was a bunch of trees, maybe ten or fifteen hourglass shaped trees, leafed out beautifully, with pinkish gold fruit.

Jimmy stopped, his mouth open. Peaches? Where did those peaches come from? Unless they were some strange New Mexican trees, which was possible.

Jimmy crossed the sandy clearing. He hopped over a broken-down stone fence and entered the orchard, for that was what it was. An ancient orchard. The trees were old, but healthy. He picked one of the tempting fruits and bit into it.

Golden sweetness rushed into his mouth. It was a peach!

He burst out of the trees to tell the others. Uncle Cully and the students still stood up on the path against the exposed striped rust, tan, and brown cliff, their backs to him. Behind him just on the edge of the orchard, Lassie whined.

"What, girl?" he asked through the peach. She sprang onto a crumbling wall and stood poised, staring out over the river. Jimmy climbed up and joined her. Across the river among oak trees was an old man. Old like the peach orchard, his face brown as the peach trunks. The intensity coming out of his eyes almost knocked Jimmy backward.

Rain People

The old man vanished, swallowed in the folds of the canyon. Before Jimmy went to tell the others, he gathered up some more ripe peaches and stuck them in his shirt. They prickled his skin.

When he and Lassie started back up, Karina was dropping down the trail, her face shining. "Did you see him?" she asked, sounding like Sarah when Sarah had seen her favorite singing band.

"Yeah! Did you?" asked Jimmy.

"I did!" She looked as if her troubles had been seized by the winds and scattered.

"Who was it?" asked Jimmy.

"I'm not exactly sure," she said, but Jimmy had a feeling she had some idea but didn't want to say.

Sarah, a sturdy branch in her hand, picked her way down behind Karina. "What's in your shirt?" Sarah asked.

"Peaches," burst out Jimmy. "Isn't that wild?"

Sarah and Karina both held out their hands, and Jimmy

distributed the fruit. Karina bit deeply, the juice running down her chin. "Nothing better than Hopi peaches," she said, her mouth full.

Sarah rubbed hers on her shirt. She said, "We studied China in school, and peaches came from China."

Karina had a funny smile on her face. "My mother is part of the Navajo nation, but several generations ago her ancestors were Hopi, so she knows some Hopi things. The Hopi people have peach orchards, and there is a story about crossing the northern seas with peach seeds."

"You mean when they immigrated?" asked Sarah. "Did they go through Ellis Island? We studied about that too."

Karina burst into peals of laughter. Lassie barked and jumped up on Karina. Jimmy was about to tell Lassie to get down. She wasn't supposed to jump up on people. But before he did anything, Karina took the collie's front paws and danced in a circle with her. Lassie laughed with Karina, her long tongue hanging out.

"The Hopi people came here thousands of years ago."

Sarah stared at her.

"That's the story," said Karina. She smiled and let Lassie drop back down to all fours. Then she ruffled Sarah's hair. "Come on. Let's take some more peaches—I think it's okay to take some—and hike up the canyon."

"Did Uncle Cully say we could?" asked Jimmy, cautiously. His uncle and the other students were still high on the canyon trail. Thin sunlight shattered down over them. He glanced up. Clouds whipped overhead in the high winds, making the the sun flicker on and off like a stuttering candle.

"Dr. Harmon—it's funny to think of him as anything but a professor—suggested we hike up the canyon. Sort of scout things out," she said. "I wanted to. A lot of what they're talking about I've seen a billion times as a kid playing in the canyons," Karina said.

So they walked through the peach orchard. Maybe fifty small trees clustered along a terraced ledge.

"This is an old orchard," said Karina. "See the drawings? See the word pictures?"

Etched on a large boulder were figures of people, arms raised, dancing around trees. Below the boulder were piles of stones. Carefully Karina collected several fist-sized stones and placed them with the others.

"Why did you do that?" asked Sarah.

"To be polite," said Karina.

So Jimmy and Sarah picked up a stone each and put them beside Karina's. Dad always told them to be polite.

"Look at Lassie," said Karina, delightedly.

The collie had a stone in her mouth. Gently she dropped the stone by the pile. "What a good, smart *perrito,*" she said.

"What did you call her?" asked Jimmy as they began to follow the path out of the orchard.

"Spanish for doggie," said Karina.

"You're all kinds of things, aren't you?" asked Sarah. "Navajo, Hopi, Spanish. My family is just plain old American."

Karina laughed. "So am I. Ancient American."

"That's right," Jimmy said. "Her family is the original American. The Harmons are from Germany. Although the Harmons have been in America for a couple hundred years."

"And you completely belong here," said Karina. "That is America. A place for many."

They crossed a low, sandy cut in the canyon that looked like a giant had taken a knife and slashed the canyon crosswise. A small pool of the Echo River flowed into the wash. Lassie drank from it while they drank from their canteens.

Sarah sat, her back to them, staring at the opposite canyon side. "Quit splashing," she yelled suddenly. Her voice echoed off the canyon walls.

"I'm not splashing," said Jimmy. The canyon whispered, *Splashing, splashing.*

Sarah wiped at her face. "Someone is splashing."

"I think it's the clouds," said Karina. "It's starting to rain."

They continued along the old trail as spatters of rain flecked them.

"Is it going to rain a lot?" asked Jimmy, holding out his hand.

Karina glanced up. "Maybe. We'll stay on this side in case the river grows large and prevents us from crossing."

"You talk like things are alive," said Sarah. "The river. The rain. The peach trees."

"Aren't they?" asked Karina. "They act more alive than some people I know."

Jimmy thought, *God did make the rain, rivers, and trees. Are they alive?* Trees could die, rivers, too, sort of. But that wasn't the same as people who have souls and a conscience. He wondered if Karina worshiped the trees, rivers, and stuff, even though she was a college student getting her masters degree.

Wasn't that a main difference of belief? Some people worshiped the creation instead of the Creator—God. Without God, the rain, trees, rivers, and all people wouldn't be here. But God was still God if there wasn't any rain, trees, rivers, or even people.

Jimmy was curious to know Karina's thoughts, how she saw the world. He didn't want to point out how he thought she was wrong, if she did worship the creation as her ancestors did, but because he cared about her, he wanted to know how she saw the world so he could understand her better.

Tower in the Clouds

The drops tumbled down sporadically. "It's raining high up," said Karina, "and evaporating before it reaches the ground."

"Weird," said Sarah. "At home it rains straight down."

They continued to climb the stony path higher and higher along the cliff wall. Occasionally one of them would yell, "Hello!" or some other word, just to hear the echo.

Close to the top of the cliff, Jimmy was too breathless to talk. Even Lassie panted.

"Rest here," said Karina, and she flopped down on an outcropping, almost like a bookshelf. Jimmy and Sarah flung themselves down on either side of Karina like bookends.

"How high are we?" asked Sarah peering over the edge. Far below was the silver thread of the Echo River.

"A thousand feet?" asked Jimmy. "It felt like about four thousand."

Karina chuckled. "I was going to say, 'You poor city kids,' but I'm as winded as you are! I'm out of shape. I've been gone too long."

"Where do you live?" asked Jimmy.

"I've been at the university for almost five years. But my family lives near Shiprock," she said.

Lassie rested her head on Jimmy's outstretched leg. He poured water into a plastic container and she lapped it up.

"See that funny-looking rock," said Sarah. Ahead, nearly at the top of the canyon, stood a very tall stone. "Let's go to it."

Karina stood and studied it through her camera's telephoto lens. "You know, Sarah," Karina said slowly, "I think you found another ruin. Doesn't it look like a tower?" She handed her camera to Jimmy.

He peered through the lens. "Sure looks like it is."

"Let's go check it out," said Karina. "Then we can tell Dr. Harmon. I know the others would like to see it, if it's what I think it is."

Jimmy wiped his backside free of clinging leaves and dust and then laughed at himself. He was going to be dirty until they got back to Grandpa's.

"I'm hungry," said Sarah.

"It won't take long to check out that tower," said Karina.

"Have a peach?" asked Jimmy. He had put five in his pack. Sarah made a face. Karina dug in her pack and handed Sarah a candy bar. "Will this help?" Karina asked.

Sarah nodded and munched happily as they continued along the rock face.

As they neared the top, the wind snapped around them. A rumble echoed down the canyon, as if a large boulder were rolling through. "Maybe it will rain," said Jimmy.

Karina nodded. "Hear the thunder?"

"It sounded like a rock falling," said Sarah.

"Thunder," said Karina.

The path twined in and out of unseen ripples in the canyon wall. After a good half hour the tower seemed almost as far away. Thunder grumbled through the canyon again, but the rain had quit falling. Only the wind stayed the same—fierce, needle sharp, and cold.

"Perhaps the storm is passing next to us," said Karina.

A raven rode the winds near them, silent and dark as the clouds. Lassie slipped past Jimmy and Karina and took the lead. *She sure needs a brushing,* thought Jimmy. No wonder all the pictures he'd seen of Indian dogs showed them with short fur.

"Just another minute now," said Karina, encouragingly.

The trail did another funny drop and twist, hiding the tower from sight. They climbed yet another rise for a good ten minutes, and the tower finally appeared.

Jimmy whistled sharply.

Karina nodded appreciatively. "Looks in good shape, doesn't it?"

The tower was square, two stories tall, and had small windows around the top. It was built on the edge of the precipice. Karina laid her palms on the bricks and pressed her forehead against the stone. "Amazing," she said. "It's just so amazing."

Jimmy wasn't sure if she meant the tower or finding it.

Quietly the trio stepped inside the typical open T-shaped door. Lassie remained outside, sniffing about.

Inside they plunged into darkness. Jimmy snapped on his small penlight. Karina put a cool hand on his wrist. "Turn it off, okay?"

Puzzled, he did as she asked. They stood for a moment. His eyes began to adjust, and he realized it wasn't so dark after all. Pale light sifted down from the small windows. Some light trickled in the door. When Lassie, her nose still to the ground, lightly hopped inside, her toenails clicked on the floor. Jimmy knelt.

"There's a painting here," he said amazed, and touched the turquoise edges defining the neat, small squares of the drawing. He ran his fingers to the edges of the painting. It was at least as big as a quilt. He tried to pick out one of the turquoise stones, but it was stuck in somehow.

Karina knelt beside him. "It's a mosaic," she whispered. "I've never seen one quite like this though."

Sarah leaned over them, her hands on Jimmy's shoulders. "It's a drawing of tree, isn't it? A peach tree?"

Karina nodded. "A spruce tree." She reached out, not to touch the small tiles, but pointed at the tree's base and near it. "Corn, with stars overhead, and clouds and raindrops."

The light level paled until the room looked as if it were in an undersea world. Outside the winds rushed like waves onto a shore.

Sarah had moved to the edge of the mosaic and said, "Look, a rainbow here."

Jimmy and Karina moved to look as Lassie whimpered and pressed against Jimmy's leg. He leaned over to stroke her. "What is it, girl?"

She barked sharply and lunged at Sarah who was closest to the northwest corner of the tower. Lassie knocked Sarah backward into Jimmy's arms as a tremendous boom shook the tower.

Stones crashed down on them. Jimmy shielded Sarah with his arms and upper body. They huddled together as more stones fell. *The sky is falling,* he thought dazedly.

Jimmy wanted to shout Karina's name, Lassie's name, but the air filled with dust and he couldn't catch his breath.

A funny metallic taste filled his mouth and a burnt smell collected in the tower. It was almost as bad as the skunk. Finally, Jimmy could take a breath again, though the burning seared his throat.

Kiva Tower

In an instant, the world filled with rain. Lassie had shoved Sarah into Jimmy's arms and they both had fallen over the upside down T-shaped doorway. Outside rain poured down by giant pitchers and monstrous buckets. Icy water pelted them, and Jimmy struggled to gain his feet and move out of the sheets of water.

Someone shouted, pulled at his shirt collar, and helped him stand and balance Sarah beside him.

"Are you okay?" Karina gasped.

Embarrassed, that he hadn't helped Karina at all, he meekly said, "I'm fine. Sarah?" He turned to his sister and stared into her face. But she flailed from him.

"Lassie! Look, she's hurt," cried Sarah. "She pushed us away and now she'd hurt."

A brilliant arc of lightning spilt the sky, and he tasted the metallic flavor again. The tower must have been struck by lightning. Had Lassie been hit?

He and Sarah rushed to the limp dog. She was lying flat

on her side, her beautiful full tail spread over the starry heavens of the mosaic.

Her eyes were open and she gazed at Jimmy. A trickle of blood, watered down by rain, wet the fur beside her ear.

Jimmy put his hands on his dog. Lassie whined softly. She was breathing. He felt for her pulse along her neck. It was beating fast. Carefully he searched her body, checking for broken bones and wounds. She only whined when he touched her head above her ear. How hard had she been hit? Dogs could get concussions, too, like people.

"What's wrong with her?" whispered Sarah.

More thunder shook the tower. Jimmy shook his head. He didn't know.

Karina knelt beside him and put her hand on Jimmy's arm. "Let's make her comfortable," suggested Karina.

Rain swished in through the door. "Now this is like Iowa. Cats and dogs," Sarah said.

Jimmy couldn't see anything through the rain. It was as if the desert had turned into an ocean.

Amazingly the roof only leaked from a couple of places. Even with Jimmy's small flashlight, they couldn't see the ceiling.

Karina said, "Lightning hit the tower, but fortunately it didn't break it up too much."

"Just Lassie," said Sarah, her eyes filling with tears. "If she hadn't jumped at me, those rocks would have hit me."

She kicked at the tumble of stones.

"Here's a blanket," said Jimmy digging in his pack. He pulled out the small square of silver—the space blanket—and his extra flannel shirt. He spread his shirt on a semi-dry portion of the floor.

"Can you sit up?" he asked Lassie. He could pick her up if he had to, but he wanted to see if she were able to move on her own.

Slowly the big collie lifted her head. Jimmy steadied her when she wobbled. Then Lassie stood up, her back hunched, and crept to the soft flannel shirt. Immediately she lay flat on her side and closed her eyes with a sigh. Jimmy unfolded the blanket and covered her.

Karina told Sarah to get everyone's canteens and hold them out the door in the rain to fill them. As Sarah did that, Karina removed some plant pods from her jacket pocket. She told Jimmy, "I was collecting these for Triangle's leg. But they should help Lassie's cut."

He agreed. So Karina took Lassie's drinking bowl and filled it with fresh rainwater. Jimmy held his dog's head up and Lassie drank a little, then wearily put her head back down. Karina dipped the beans in the water, crushed them with a small rock, then gently parted the dog's fur, laying the fresh pulp on the jagged cut. A lump the size of an egg had risen next to her ear.

"What plant is that?" asked Jimmy.

"Castor beans," she said. "They're poisonous to eat, but good for putting on wounds."

The cold floor sucked at the warmth from Jimmy's body. He started shivering. "Is it getting colder or is it me?" he asked.

"Colder," said Karina. Her teeth were beginning to chatter. Sarah stood, her arms wrapped around herself.

So what do we do? wondered Jimmy. *Maybe I should go for help?* He wondered if he could make it back along the cliff edge, the path now slick with rain.

Sarah suddenly squealed. "It's hailing," she cried.

Sure enough. Ice chunks pinged outside, bouncing on the rocks. A couple rattled in the door.

Thank you, God, Jimmy thought, *that we aren't in the hail.* Hail that big could kill you.

Sarah picked up an ice chunk and threw it back outside. "Stay outside," she said to the hail, then turned to them. "I wish we could make a fire or something. I'm freezing."

Of course by now everything outside would be soaked. Jimmy poked his hand into the corners of the tower where some debris lay—mostly leaves, a few twigs.

"Careful," warned Karina. "Snakes or scorpions could be hiding in there." She held the poultice on Lassie's wound with her fingers, and with her other hand gently rubbed the collie's neck and shoulders.

"Scorpions, ick," said Sarah.

After that Jimmy kicked at small piles of branches and rocks with his boots. "Here's a little bit of wood. Not enough for a fire, though."

Sarah looked out the door and said, "I can see a couple of sticks close."

"Bring them in," said Karina, leaning over Lassie. "Put something over your head though. We don't need you getting brained by hail."

Sarah emptied her backpack and held it over her head. She darted out and back with three sticks in her hands. "Isn't it funny?" she commented. "These sticks have feathers tied to them."

Karina looked up and gasped. "Sarah, put them back, quickly!"

Sarah, startled, dropped them and they bounced onto the stone floor.

Jimmy gawked as Karina sprang up and gently lifted the feathered sticks. Karina disappeared outside without even covering her head.

When she darted back in, water sheened off her jacket and she shook her wet hair.

Sarah, in the dim light, had a scared look on her face as she asked, "What were they?" Jimmy couldn't help but think of the staff Moses had in the desert and how it turned into a snake.

Karina said, "They're *pahos*, prayer sticks of the Hopi."

Sarah still looked scared. "I didn't know. I'm sorry. Is something bad going to happen?"

Jimmy wanted to say, "Something bad has already happened. Look at Lassie!" But he didn't.

Karina gave her a tender smile. "No, no. You didn't know. It just startled me to see them. That's all. But I think we won't use them for the fire."

The hail and rain combo switched back to only rain. The rain continued to pour down. A pool was growing in the far corner from one of the bigger leaks.

Jimmy tried to think what Dad would do in a situation like this. He'd pray. So Jimmy asked, "Do you mind if I pray for Lassie and us too?"

Karina turned her large eyes on him. "Of course not. Please do."

So he did, asking that all of them be kept safe, that Lassie would be okay. Also he asked that if they were doing anything disrespectful to the Indians' tower or prayer sticks or whatever, that the Hopi people would forgive them for their ignorance. Jimmy meant that with all his heart. Just because they believed differently than he did, he didn't want to do anything rude.

When he ended the prayer and opened his eyes, Karina was looking at him. "Thank you," said Karina softly. "You know, I don't know a lot about my Hopi heritage. Just scattered things. So your prayer applies to me, too."

Lassie seemed to be sleeping. Her eyes were closed and she breathed evenly. Jimmy stroked her under the space blanket and gently untangled burrs from her coat.

Sarah scratched around with a stick, cleaning dirt from the mosaic. Every few minutes she did jumping jacks. "To keep warm," she explained. Jimmy wished he had her energy. His teeth were chattering. The rain had seeped through all his clothes.

They listened as the rain lashed the canyon. The light faded, and the sun was held hostage in the storm clouds.

Okay, God, thought Jimmy. *What now?*

Sarah tripped over Jimmy's leg, intent on her cleaning. A minute later she said, "Look at this, part of the stone floor is missing."

Karina rose and looked. "Let me see your flashlight, Jimmy," said Karina. He handed it to her and watched, questioningly.

Suddenly Karina passed the flashlight to Sarah, leaned over, and with a grunt, pulled up what looked like bare dirt but was actually a slab of stone.

"A cave!" exclaimed Sarah.

"Not a cave," said Karina with a funny tremor in her voice. "A kiva."

Lovely and Sightless

A key-what?" asked Sarah.

Jimmy had heard the word before and thought it was some kind of ceremonial room, but that was about it.

"A kiva," said Karina. "It's a little like a church."

"An underground church?" asked Jimmy. "Cool." He'd have to mention that to Dad. What a good idea! Especially during a tornado watch.

"Help me move this stone away," said Karina. Jimmy helped her drag the heavy slab of stone off to the side. A dark square yawned open. "There should be a ladder," said Karina, reaching down into the black hole. Jimmy shone his little flashlight beam into the square. The hole dropped forever, and like the ceiling, light didn't touch the bottom or sides. Karina kept fishing around after he clicked off his light.

"How did you know there was a kiva under that stone?" asked Sarah.

"I didn't know," Karina grunted, reaching so far Jimmy

93

was afraid she'd fall in. He poised, ready to grab her.

"Here it is," Karina said and pulled a wooden ladder up to the opening of the hole.

"In here we'll be out of the rain, and at least we'll be protected from the temperature changes," said Karina. "I have a nasty feeling we're going to be stuck here tonight."

"It's almost a full moon tonight," said Jimmy. "We could see to go back—"

"—if the skies clear up," finished Karina.

Then there was Lassie who was injured. Jimmy glanced at the collie. She had sat up, the silver space blanket fallen off, during the excitement of opening the kiva.

"Lassie," said Sarah. "Are you feeling better?"

The dog stood and didn't move for a moment as if gathering her strength. Then she stepped toward Jimmy, her tail wagging gently. "That's a good girl," said Jimmy. He was on the opposite side of the kiva entry from her. He started to move around the hole, his arms open, when Lassie walked straight toward him.

And walked straight into the hole. She fell so fast that Jimmy only had time to grab at her tail. A clump of fur tore loose in his hand. Sarah screamed and rushed to edge.

The big dog thumped into the darkness with a yelp.

"Lassie!" Jimmy cried out. How could she have not seen the hole?

Jimmy swiftly climbed down the ladder. He clenched

his little flashlight in his teeth and prayed that the ladder would hold his weight and that Lassie was okay.

The ladder let him down next to a low brick fire wall. A large stone-ringed fire pit was directly under the hole. The girls' faces loomed above him. He carefully climbed off the ladder and turned the light onto Lassie.

She sat up with a low whine. She'd fallen in the fire pit onto a huge pile of soft ashes. Thank God. Jimmy helped her out onto the earthen floor beside the pit.

"Is she okay?" called Sarah.

"I don't know," he said, running his hands over her body, brushing off ashes. "She landed in the fire pit, on top of the ashes." Jimmy held his shaking dog. *She's scared,* he thought.

"I'm coming down," said Karina.

"Me, too," said Sarah.

"First drop the packs down to me, would you?" said Karina.

The girls brought down their packs. As Sarah climbed down, Karina guiding her gently.

Karina poked around in the ash-gray light. "There's firewood here," she said. She lit a branch torch and handed it to Sarah. "Be our light pole, okay?"

Sarah held the torch near Jimmy and Lassie as Jimmy resettled Lassie on her bed of his shirt. The dog sat down and leaned against Jimmy. Karina carried an arm-load of branches to the fire pit and coaxed a fire into being.

"Why did Lassie fall?" asked Sarah.

Jimmy gently stroked his dog's head. "I'm not sure," he said, not wanting to believe what flickered in his brain.

As the fire brightened the kiva, Jimmy slowly passed his hand in front of Lassie's eyes. She didn't blink. He did it again and again. "Oh Lassie," he finally whispered. Karina took the torch from Sarah.

One last test. Jimmy shone the flashlight into Lassie's eyes. Her pupils remained large, unchanged, not dilating. "She can't see," he said, almost not believing his own eyes.

"What do you mean?" whispered Sarah. "She was bleeding from her ear, not her eyes."

"I don't know," Jimmy said, "but she sure didn't see the hole, or my hand, or the flashlight."

Karina crouched beside the lovely, sightless collie. "When she was hit by those falling stones, they must have hurt her sight in her brain."

Jimmy ran his hands over her neck, her shoulders, her ribs. She licked his hands. "We have to get her to a vet," said Jimmy.

"I don't know how we can do that until the rain stops," said Karina. "It's nearly night. What if the hail starts again? And with the lightning striking so close, we could be hit again."

Karina sat back on her heels, biting her lip. "I could go

for help, if you two promise to stay here."

"We're supposed to stay together," said Sarah. "That's what Uncle Cully told us before Jimmy and I left with him—the buddy system."

Jimmy met Karina's gaze. "She's right. We shouldn't separate ourselves."

"But Lassie . . ." began Karina.

"It's okay," said Jimmy, not feeling as strong as he wished he was. "God will take care of her. I mean, we should do what we can, but I don't think we should risk our lives. We couldn't leave from base camp tonight anyway. Maybe Lassie is in shock or something. Her eyesight could come back." But he didn't really believe that.

Thunder shook the cliff. Even in the kiva they felt the boom. A small stone clattered down the hole and fell into the fire. Over the rattle of the rain, the echo of the thunder came back to them. *Echo Cliffs,* thought Jimmy.

The storm, or perhaps it was more than one storm, seemed to shift down the canyon, then work its way back up.

Lassie whined softly and looked up. Jimmy started to reassure her that it was just a storm, when a soft light played overhead. Not brittle, stabbing lightning flashes, but as if someone were holding a candle or a branch torch.

Overhead, a shadow of a figure floated across the kiva entrance.

The Cloud People

Lassie gave a low, but welcoming bark. She wagged her tail. Jimmy swallowed hard as the shadow vanished and the soft glow was extinguished.

"Who's there?" hollered Karina. She jumped as thunder crashed, sounding like monster cymbals. When the lightning streaks split the sky and darted into the tower with weird, jagged shadows, Karina hastily climbed up the ladder. Jimmy was humiliated but relieved that it was Karina and not him climbing to face the unknown.

Lassie continued to thump her tail in an erratic way. Was more than her sight injured? . . . Her personality? . . . Her judgement, which was always so true and clear?

Jimmy wanted to yell in anger that it wasn't fair! But he didn't. He steadily stroked his dog.

Karina peered back down, her wet hair dripping into the fire. "No one is around now, at least from what I can tell," she added wryly.

"Come back, Karina," said Jimmy pleadingly. "Don't get

all wet again." But she had vanished.

Jimmy tried to smile at his sister who was clearing a spot for herself and curling up almost like a puppy.

Karina clattered back down, her long hair running with water. She was soaked.

"Karina!" protested Sarah. "You'll get sick."

"Not me," she said, "I'm tough." She stalked around the kiva that was about the size of the Harmon's living room at home.

"There ought to be a ventilation tunnel," said Karina as she searched. "I want to check to be sure it's clear." She took another branch and lit a torch.

Karina walked around the far edges of the cave, her torch casting twisted shadows. All around the kiva were empty shelves embedded in the rocks. *What did they hold?* Jimmy wondered.

"Here it is," said Karina, stopping behind him and Lassie. Her torch illuminated a small opening. "I'll be right back," she said and then disappeared into it.

"She's brave," said Sarah. "I'd be terrified."

Jimmy almost said, "Well, she does know kivas and stuff," then he thought of Sarah's fear of Echo Canyon's tale and said quietly, "You're right, Sarah. She is brave."

The torch flame in Karina's hand was wild and unruly. Then it disappeared.

Sarah and Jimmy looked at each other in the light of the

fire. Lassie lay with her head on Jimmy's lap. The big collie didn't act restless or wary, but Jimmy kept telling himself that he couldn't rely on *her* now. She was injured. He must be the one *she* could rely on.

"Has the rain stopped? I can't hear it," asked Sarah, cocking her head and staring up at the smoke twisting through the hole.

"Probably not. The stone in these caves is like a sound room, it's so thick."

The torch light gleamed again, and seconds later Karina popped her wet head back out. "The tunnel's clear," she said, smiling. "It also goes outside. Obviously, it's still pouring," she said, wringing her hair. She took off her jacket and laid it carefully on the ground near the fire.

"I guess God answered the prayers of your people," Sarah observed.

"How's that?" asked Karina, coming close to the fire, her hands held out.

"Because it's raining," explained Sarah. "You said they've been praying."

"Oh, yeah," said Karina. "But I'm not sure they're praying to the same gods." Karina chuckled as the orange flames danced and the kiva warmed.

Jimmy asked, "Do you believe in God, in Jesus?"

Karina sat back on her heels. "My father's family, the Peñas, mostly do. But my mother's family, the ones who follow the Navajo way, believe in spirits. The Hopi people believe that Kachinas, or spirits of their ancestors, provide rain, life really. They are known as the Cloud People."

A chill circled Jimmy despite the warming fire. *What if that's what we saw?* A Kachina. He'd seen Kachina dolls, strange human forms with beautiful masks, but some had almost scary masks.

Sarah snuggled down in her jacket. "But Kachinas aren't real, right?"

Karina hesitated. "Well, yes, the Hopis . . . we . . . believe they are real."

"So do the Kachinas talk to Jesus about making rain and stuff?" persisted Sarah.

Karina smiled again. "No, Sarah." Then she hesitated. "This is getting complicated," she said, looking at Jimmy. He could tell Karina was worried about saying the wrong thing.

"Sarah," Jimmy said, "the Hopi people don't believe in Jesus or God at all. They have their own beliefs."

"Well, all I know is when I get in trouble and I need help," she said, "I can pray to God and He helps me out. He answers my prayers."

Lassie moved under Jimmy's hand, and he petted her until she relaxed and seemed to fall asleep.

"The Hopis believe in Kachinas because they help the Hopis," Karina responded.

"I think Sarah is trying to say that she . . . we . . . have a personal friendship with our God. We can talk to Him on a one-to-one basis, as Dad would say," Jimmy said. He wished Dad were there. He was good at explaining complicated stuff in a simple way. "Do you have a personal relationship with a Kachina?"

Karina said thoughtfully, "No, the Kachinas sort of get inside of people, but not just anybody. Only our initiated people can have this experience."

Jimmy was starting to feel real uneasy.

"I haven't been initiated yet," she continued a little sadly. "I'm sort of caught between worlds. Sometimes it's a good thing, being Spanish, Navajo, and Hopi. But sometimes I don't belong anywhere."

Jimmy heard himself say, "Anyone can belong to Jesus, and you don't have to be from a special tribe or anything. It's like being adopted. You are totally accepted into His family forever. Dad says you become an heir."

Karina drew in the sand with a twig. "That sounds great," she said. "I've spent a lot of time wanting to belong."

"You can belong," he said gently, watching the struggle going on within her. Jimmy knew that Karina would have to give up part of her heritage, her beliefs, to follow Jesus. Dad always told him that people couldn't find real happiness in their lives because they wanted to be committed in too many areas, to too many things.

"The Bible says you can't serve two masters, Jim," Dad

would say. "You can't be a Christian on Sunday and serve your own interests the rest of the week. Being a Christian means that you are committed to Christ and His Word every day. No person or thing can come between you and God."

As he sat there, Jimmy realized for the first time in his life that he had never had to give up a belief to come to Christ. All of his life he had been in the Harmon home and had trusted his dad completely to lead him in the right direction. But what if he had grown up believing something else? Would he be able to just decide one day that what he had believed to that point was wrong?

Karina sighed a little. The three of them sat wrapped in warm silence. Sarah yawned widely.

"Karina," said Jimmy. "Who do you think was in the tower?"

She bent her sleek head, still drawing in the sand. "I didn't see anyone."

"But there was someone," he said. "Don't you have an idea who it might be?"

Karina finally glanced up at him. "Yes, I do."

His heart chilled within him because suddenly he knew what she was going to say. "Who?" he asked anyway.

"A Kachina."

Sarah gasped and hugged herself. "Jimmy, they aren't real, are they?"

A Special Old Man

Karina avoided Jimmy's eyes as if to tell him, "Your call. Tell what you must."

A sudden pang took Jimmy. Was this how his parents felt? Wanting to comfort, yet knowing the truth wasn't always warm and friendly.

"Sarah," he said, kindly. "It's okay. No Kachina is going to get you. Jesus is stronger and His Spirit is in you."

Some of the tenseness left Sarah's face. "But if there is one around here . . ." she said and stopped.

Karina said, "We believe that Kachinas take care of the Hopi people. When children are little they give them gifts."

"Really?" asked Sarah. "What kinds of gifts?"

"Little, perfectly carved Kachina dolls; little carved lightning bolts with beautiful colors; bows and arrows; handmade baskets. They are," she paused, her forehead wrinkled in thought, "not exactly sacred, but symbolic to help the child remember who he is."

"Did you ever get gifts from the Kachinas?" asked Jimmy.

"Once," she said, "when I was quite little. I was visiting some cousins. My mother had been very sick after having my sister, so I went to stay with Hopi family. It was early February because my sister was born January 29."

Sarah wriggled impatiently. "What presents did you get?"

Karina laughed as Jimmy said, "Sarah, maybe she isn't supposed to say."

"No, it's fine," said Karina. "I have them hanging on my dorm wall. I received, if I can pronounce them properly, a *Qa'okatsina,* the Corn Kachina, and the *Angwushahay'i,* the Crow Mother Kachina. I got a little coiled basket, too."

"Wow," said Sarah.

Jimmy gave Karina a knowing look. Then Jimmy said with a laugh, "Can you tell what my sister likes?"

As they completely warmed in the fire, they ate more peaches that Jimmy had picked in the orchard. They talked of the rains and the canyon. Karina told them about a horse she had when she was Sarah's age and how she would ride her horse far, far into the desert and never see anyone. "Only turkey vultures, ravens, and wild sheep."

Then they fell asleep. A couple times Jimmy half awoke, thinking he saw a large shadow on the wall. He would freeze, terrified an angry spirit would grab him. But then he'd tell himself, *No, it is the the shadow of my friend, the Holy Spirit.* Gradually he'd fall back to sleep comforted.

Once when he awoke, the fire was spitting low. He put

more branches into the fire until the flames chased back the darkness to the edges of the kiva.

His gaze rested on the dark tunnel. Suddenly he realized the man, the Kachina, whomever he'd seen, well, this was his kiva. Was it right they had taken it over? Were they being totally rude? He felt bad it had taken him so long to think of that.

Slowly he rose. Lassie staggered up beside him, and together they crept to the deeply shadowed tunnel.

Jimmy whispered down the tunnel, feeling foolish, but needing to say it, "I hope you don't mind us borrowing your kiva. We appreciate getting out of the rain. Thank you." He wished he knew the Hopi word for thank you. *"Gracias,"* he added. Maybe the man knew Spanish.

Karina stirred in her sleep at his words, so he fell silent. He stood a few minutes more and prayed for their safety.

Lassie whined and stepped into the tunnel. "No, girl," he said. "Stay here." He dropped to his knees and put his arms around the collie. As he looked past her into the tunnel, in the shadowy firelight, he saw the legs of a man.

Jimmy's heart stopped pounding and he wanted to run, but he couldn't move. Lassie, Lassie, poor rattle-brained Lassie, just gently wagged her tail, like everything was okay, like they weren't caught in a canyon in a thunder storm, at night, with an unknown man.

Jimmy lifted his gaze to search the shadows. A man's

face loomed out of the darkness. An old man with a brown, wrinkled face. He stepped closer. It was the old man from the orchard! Jimmy was sure. Those eyes, those intense, blazing eyes. Not cruel, or mean, but strong and trustworthy.

The man wore a simple flannel shirt, with jeans and boots. He wasn't wet though. For that Jimmy was thankful. The man had another place to stay and be dry.

Lassie boldly walked to the old man. He bent, and stroked the collie's head. Then he reached into his pocket and pulled out a small leather bag. He held it up to show Jimmy. He unfolded it, and inside was a pile of dried herbs, berries, and tiny pieces of bark.

Then he offered the bag, folded back up, to Jimmy. Jimmy held out his hand and the man pressed it into his hand. Then he pointed at Lassie, mimicking swallowing.

"But what is it for?" whispered Jimmy.

The man bent, lifted a stone, pretended it fell on his head, and pointed to his eyes. Then he pointed to Lassie. Jimmy caught his breath. How could he know? How could he—

The man took out another small bag, and poured the contents into his palm. Then he held his hand under Lassie's mouth. Jimmy knew he should be afraid, should pull Lassie away. Maybe he was poisoning her. He knew that the man was trying to help, rather, he would help.

Lassie knew too. She bowed her head and licked the dried herbs from his palm. Jimmy didn't think normally his dog would eat dried plants, berries, and tree bark.

When Lassie was done, the man rose, came close, put his hand on Jimmy's shoulder, and squeezed gently. Then he waved Jimmy back to the kiva, and he turned around and vanished into the dark tunnel.

Jimmy started after him, to try and explain that he could stay in the kiva, too, that it was all right, but then he thought better of rushing off into a dark tunnel on a stormy night.

He stepped back into the kiva. It was bright as day compared to the tunnel.

Karina opened her eyes. "Jimmy?" she asked sleepily.

"I saw the old man again." He sat beside her. Lassie curled between the two of them.

"I thought I heard your voice," she said. "Was he dressed like a Kachina?"

Jimmy shook his head. "He just had on jeans and a flannel shirt. He didn't talk to me, but he gave Lassie this." He showed her the bag of herbs. "He knew about the rock hitting her on the head and that she was blind."

Karina studied the herbs. "I wonder if he's one of the Indian doctors."

For the first time since they found the tower and the kiva, Jimmy wasn't scared, not even a little.

"I think God sent him to us," said Jimmy.

Karina gave him a crooked smile. "You do, do you?"

"Yup," he said, then fell asleep until morning.

The Roaring River

When Jimmy awoke the fire was nearly out. The girls were still sleeping. He wanted to see if the rain had quit so they could get Lassie and themselves back to base camp.

"Lassie, stay," he told her. Jimmy changed the nearly dead batteries in his flashlight, then ducked into the tunnel. Would he meet the old man this morning? He hoped so. He wanted to know more about him and how he knew about Lassie.

He followed the brief twists and turns of the tunnel. Morning light blazed in the exit and drenched him. He blinked in the sharp light and had to wait a minute until his eyes quit watering.

The tunnel opened onto the canyon wall, a narrow path teetering on the edge of the cliff. Good thing he hadn't gone all the way out last night. How had the old man done it?

Lots of practice, Jimmy thought. The stones were smooth and slick from the rain. To the east and as far as he could see over the stone walls, the sky was a hazy blue. Yet directly overhead the clouds boiled the color of bruised grapes.

A huge, steady roaring began to filter into his consciousness, and he realized the small Echo stream had transformed into a wild river, foaming brown and leaping and plunging like angry longhorn cattle.

What if they had crossed over the little river? They'd be stuck on the other side for who knows how long. At least now they could go back to Uncle Cully. *He must be worried sick,* thought Jimmy. He hated worrying his uncle.

When he returned to the kiva, the girls were awake. Lassie had stayed and was stretching and yipping at Sarah, who was rubbing her eyes and saying, "I'm starved. Has the rain stopped? Even if it hasn't I think we ought to try and go back."

"Do I look wet?" asked Jimmy, grinning.

"Maybe a little washed out," said Karina.

Lassie barked, as if laughing at the pun. Jimmy made a face and said, "It's not raining, but it looks like it might start again any time."

"Let's get going then," said Sarah. "I hope Uncle Cully isn't mad."

"Why should he be?" asked Jimmy. "He's probably scared."

"Sometimes I get mad when I'm scared," said Sarah.

Karina teased, "He won't be mad or scared. After all, I'm with you."

Jimmy almost added, "More importantly, God is with

us," but he knew that Karina wouldn't completely understand that statement. Lassie was with them too, but with her injury, Jimmy didn't know how much help she could be.

They stuffed their belongings into their packs. Jimmy and Karina hoisted Lassie up the ladder. She struggled and scratched his arms and neck, scared. "It's okay, girl," he panted as he dragged her up. Karina pulled from the top, and they flopped the big dog onto the tower floor and caught their breath for a moment.

When they headed out, cold sunshine greeted them.

"It's another world," said Sarah. Trees, bushes, and rocks shone as if freshly polished. The sky was the color of deep turquoise, and the clouds, though threatening, changed hues—violet, gray, silver, and black.

"Look at the top of the tower," said Karina. They turned on the trail. The reddish bricks on one edge of the flattop roof were shot through with black lashes from the lightning.

As they climbed the trail, Karina looked again through her camera telephoto lens. "That roof is made from timbers," she said. "We were lucky it didn't catch fire."

Jimmy thanked God. Their guardian angels must have been working overtime.

They hurried back, not stopping to look at much. Lassie walked easily enough, not hesitating as long as Jimmy were near. She seemed to follow him by sound and scent.

Following them the whole way was the harsh roar of

Lassie™: Danger at Echo Cliffs

the river, unleashed and running wild through the canyon below. They paused briefly a couple times to watch the waters jetting along the swollen riverbed hundreds of feet below them.

During a water break, Jimmy gave Lassie the herbs that the old man had given him and stuffed the empty leather bag into his pocket. She ate the herbs willingly, which surprised him. The lump next to her ear was still tender and she pulled away if anyone touched it, but the jagged cut was already healing.

"That Echo river water is wilder than the Mississippi," said Sarah. "I mean when the Mississippi floods it is scary, but down there the water is crazy."

"I'm just glad we didn't go across it yesterday before the rain came," said Jimmy.

Suddenly Karina put her hand to her mouth and turned to them with terrified eyes. "Oh no," she said in a frightened whisper. "Oh no," and she leaned against the stone cliff as if she couldn't stand up anymore.

Message Bag

What is it?" asked Jimmy. It was bad enough Lassie was hurt, but if Karina were getting sick, he didn't think he could cope.

"The wash we crossed," began Karina, and she choked out a couple of desperate laughs and slid down the rock wall onto the path.

"The wash?" Jimmy asked stupidly. He had an image of his mother hanging out the laundry, the sheets and shirts snapping in the wind.

Sudden horror took Sarah. Her legs collapsed and she plopped down on the trail where she'd been standing. "You mean the other dry riverbed we crossed," said Sarah. "It won't be dry anymore."

Understanding finally smacked into Jimmy. "Are you sure?" he asked. "How can you be sure?"

"I can't believe it didn't occur to me," Karina said between dry laughs that sounded more and more like hard sobs. "How stupid can I get?"

Lassie nosed under Sarah's arm. "Maybe it won't be too wide?" said Sarah, hopefully, her arm around Lassie's neck.

"We better go see," said Jimmy. He held out his hand. Before Karina took it, she dropped her face into Lassie's ruff and murmured something in Spanish, then she said in English, "Look at her comfort me when she is the one who is blind." Then Karina took Jimmy's hand and he pulled her to her feet.

Jimmy didn't say anything, but his throat constricted. Lassie was brave, braver than anyone he knew, including adults, even his mom and dad. Dad would say how Lassie wore the armor of God, that she was fearless.

He pulled Sarah back up, too, and they continued along the trail, wind pushing them from behind. After fifteen minutes, the rushing noise intensified. As they came to a rise, they stopped at the top.

The dry wash had erupted into a foaming band of dark water.

"Oh great," said Sarah. "I was hoping it wouldn't be so big." The water was a good twenty feet across. "What are we supposed to do? Fly across it?" she asked and kicked some dirt into the swirling water.

The river raced along faster than a galloping horse. Jimmy was amazed how fast the river grew. Just overnight it had become impassable.

A couple of uprooted tree trunks, ducking and diving,

whirled past. No way could they cross by swimming. The current was a killer, not to mention all the debris that would assail them if they dared to try.

"There's Dr. Harmon!" shouted Karina. Jimmy and Sarah jumped up and down, waving. Lassie, as if understanding, barked and wagged her tail hopefully.

Uncle Cully waved back. They could see him moving his mouth, but his words were tangled into the noise of the rushing water and pulled away from them.

If only we could talk a minute, thought Jimmy. At least Uncle Cully would see they were okay. Except Lassie. How could he let his uncle know? If only he had a huge sheet of paper to write on. Too bad he couldn't write a message on the rocks. What had the Indians used to make paints?

Then he had an idea. He pulled out the leather bag. If he could write a note, put a rock in the bag, then throw it across the river, they could at least communicate with Uncle Cully. He thought he could throw that far. He had a pretty good arm from baseball.

"Do you have any paper?" Jimmy asked Karina.

"In my notebook. Why?"

"I think I can throw this bag with a message inside across the river. I'll put a stone in it to weigh it down."

"Anything's worth a try," said Karina. She took a small note pad out of her backpack and handed him a pencil.

Jimmy wrote a quick note, that they were okay, just

hungry, but that Lassie had been hit on the head and was blind from it.

Would a rescue helicopter come for a dog? A hurt dog? He sort of doubted it.

Jimmy gave the note to Karina who wrote a line, then Sarah wrote, too. Jimmy searched for the right shaped stone. Smaller than a baseball, but not too small. He then tightly bound the note with a hacky-sack sized stone. He wished he had a slingshot, like David had when he fought Goliath. That would help give the message a boost.

"Okay, here goes," said Jimmy. Lassie started to follow him. "Hold her, Sarah. I'm afraid she'll knock me off balance."

Lassie whined nervously, but Sarah soothed her with gentle words, and Karina murmured in Spanish. The collie relaxed, but remained intent, listening.

Jimmy hunted for a small hill or boulder to stand on near the shore. He walked upriver and found a large stone about two feet high. He hoped the added height would help him.

He waved until Uncle Cully walked upstream and was parallel to him.

Jimmy was more into running than baseball or football, but he wasn't exactly wimpy. Fortunately it was his left shoulder he'd hurt when Geometry unloaded him, and he was right handed. That fall seemed ages ago.

He threw off his backpack and warmed up his arm. He threw overhand, praying, as the small leather bag sailed over the angry, surging water. Jimmy was almost afraid to watch, but he made himself.

The leather bag landed in the sand inches from the rippling water line. Uncle Cully snatched it up, and Jimmy sighed with relief. He jumped off the boulder and ran back to Sarah, Karina, and Lassie.

He dug his fingers into Lassie's thick, soft fur, trying to think of a way to cross the cold, boiling river. As they waited for Uncle Cully to respond, a few drops of rain splattered into the damp dust.

Karina held out her hand, palm upturned and sighed. "We are in for more rain," she said.

"Where does this part of the river start?" Jimmy asked.

"I don't know, but probably in the mountains."

Too far to walk around it then.

If they could string a rope across the river, perhaps they could cross. But that was really tricky. If any of them fell into the river, certainly that person would be killed.

A few minutes later, Uncle Cully positioned himself across from them, indicated he was going to return the message bag, then threw it. It spattered into the sand beside Lassie. She jumped.

"Poor thing," cried Sarah. "She didn't know it was coming."

Jimmy picked up the bag and let Lassie sniff it. She barked happily. She knew Uncle Cully's scent. She stood up, eagerly sniffing the air for him.

"Sorry, girl," said Jimmy. "We can't get to him right now."

She barked several more times, then settled down.

Jimmy opened the note and read:

Karina, Jim, Sarah,

We're all fine, too. Just wet. I'll go back to the base camp and get some supplies for you. Maybe we can toss them across the water, attached to a rope (if I can find one long enough—tie some together). I think I should send a couple of the guys back for help. I'm wary of sending Decker. His sense of direction is disturbing. Do you have a dry place to stay?

Love, Uncle Cully.

Jimmy signaled a yes answer to Uncle Cully.

"They probably should go for help," said Karina. "Being out here isn't so great."

"I think it's raining more," said Sarah, and Jimmy wondered how this had gotten so complicated so fast.

Rope Tricks

Thunder rumbled down the canyon, echoing off the stone walls. How much had those walls heard in a thousand years? Jimmy's brain churned, like branches caught in a fast river. Wasn't life like this canyon, echoing the same words over and over? Wasn't it true that everything you did was reflected, echoed onto others? Just like the Bible said: What you sow, you reap. What you say will be echoed back.

Jimmy knew that no matter what obstacles he faced, no matter what he sowed in life, the most important thing was to keep the communication flowing between him and God.

Mom had said something one morning when they were eating breakfast that made Jimmy think. Sarah had brought up her so-called friends who never seemed to be around when she needed them.

"Well, Sarah," Mom had said. "Do you work at being a good friend?" Without waiting for an answer, she continued. "You know friends are there for you if they know they can count on you being there for them. That kind of trust takes time and effort—commitment. If you expect your friends to be committed to you, you have to be committed to them."

I wonder if the same thing works with God. Jimmy smiled, knowing Dad would like the idea for a sermon. He'd remember to tell him when they got home.

He looked at the foaming river. *If we ever get home.*

Now Jimmy, he told himself, *Jesus calmed the Sea of Galilee which was a million times bigger than this wash.* The disciples with Jesus had panicked, so Jimmy decided he wouldn't panic. *Yeah, right!* he thought. He'd try not to panic and wait to see what God wanted him to do.

So he sprawled in the damp sand, realizing how hungry he was. His stomach was turning inside out.

An hour or so later, Uncle Cully, Lyle, Connor, and Petra appeared at the river, waving and shouting wordless sentences.

Sarah and Lassie waited under a nearby cluster of cottonwood trees. Karina and Jimmy stood on the raging shoreline, Jimmy gripping the leather bag, silently thanking God again for that old man. He wondered if the old man knew a way across the river. If they could find him again. Or rather, if he would allow himself to be seen by them. Of course, the old man didn't act as if he knew English.

Connor threw the end of a rope, tied to a saddlebag. Jimmy doubted he'd be able to throw it back. It weighed a good ten pounds, maybe more. Jimmy opened the bag which was filled with supplies and another note.

"Food!" he shouted and handed out granola bars all around. Jimmy gave Lassie two dog bones which she wolfed down. *At least she is eating,* he thought. That's always a good sign.

The note read:

Everybody,

Can you tie the rope to a low, strong tree branch? We'll try to send more supplies to you by a pulley system. If the rope seems strong enough, maybe we can use it to get you all across.

Love, Uncle Cully.

Jimmy quickly ate crackers and peanut butter and thought nothing had every tasted so good.

Then he and Karina examined the cottonwood trees. "How about this branch?" asked Karina. It was sturdy, close to the thick trunk, near the water, and low on the tree.

"Okay by me," he said. He swung onto the branch, about four feet high, and sat astride it. Ouch. He was sore from riding. Wouldn't it be nice to sit in a hot bathtub?

This rope is your ticket to that hot bathtub, he told himself.

Karina flipped the rope up to him. He tied a bowline knot with a backup knot, then sat a moment on the branch, looking down at his collie. She usually barked at him when he was up a tree. But today she couldn't see him there.

Then he jumped off and waved to show he was finished. Uncle Cully and Connor climbed up a corner of the canyon, across from the cottonwood trees. The higher they could get the rope, the better the pulley system would work. Jimmy watched them tie on an additional rope.

Connor carefully scaled the cliff, virtually rock climbing, toes and fingers digging into cracks in the stone until he reached a stout, jutting rock about thirty feet up. Then Connor tied the other end of the rope around the rock.

Lyle and Petra stood at the foot of the cliff with another saddlebag bulging with supplies. Uncle Cully cut a length of rope, fashioned a loop, then handed it up to Connor, still perched on the rock face. Connor tied the loop to the rope running across the river and to the saddlebags.

"Here it comes," shouted Jimmy as Connor shoved the bags on their way.

The saddlebags bumped along the rope, hanging up on knots. Connor jerked at the line until the bags moved again.

"Come on, come on," begged Sarah.

"I'm not so sure I want to slide down that rope," said Karina. "I think they'll have to make some improvements first."

The rope drooped more and more as the bag came closer, and the edge of the saddlebag skimmed the water.

Jimmy hastily yanked off his hiking boots, rolled up his jeans, and waded knee deep into the water. He held the rope up in one hand and grabbed for the saddlebags. The current snatched furiously at him, almost making him lose his balance. And he was only knee deep!

Karina grabbed his arm and helped haul him and the bags out of the river. The rain had started falling again.

"Why don't you take Sarah and Lassie back to the kiva," said Jimmy. "No reason for all of us to get wet. I can find my way back okay."

Karina hesitated, but then agreed. She and Sarah took the saddlebag of food, no note this time, and together they walked down the path.

Lassie didn't want to leave Jimmy, but he told her, "Go with Sarah." So she meekly followed, her nose against Sarah's knee.

Uncle Cully had to cut another loop for the second bag, this time a daypack. Jimmy left his boots off and stood on the shoreline, his hand on the rope. He was shivering. His feet felt like ice blocks.

Connor sent the daypack bumping down the knotted rope line. When the pack was about a third of the way across, the rope suddenly tore out of Jimmy's hand, burning his palm.

The broken rope ends snapped in the current. Just like that, the pack and some of the rope were gone.

Jimmy slumped. He hoped nothing too important had been in the bag. Across the stream Connor lifted his shoulders and his arms, as if to say, "Oh well, what can you do?" and he climbed back down the rock corner.

As Jimmy reeled in what was left of the rope on his side, he realized the mishap may have been a blessing in disguise. What if the rope had held for several bags, then broken when one of them had tried to cross?

Jimmy hunched over the paper Karina had left with him and wrote a quick note telling Uncle Cully that they were going back to the kiva where it was warm and dry. He added that they could meet again in the morning. He tossed the leather bag to the other side.

When Uncle Cully finished reading the note, he held up a notebook page that read OKAY in big black letters. Within seconds, the rain beat the paper into black mush.

Jimmy waved good-bye and hurried back to the kiva.

When he climbed down the ladder, a good fire was crackling. Thank God and the old man for the firewood. Both girls were asleep, but Lassie wasn't there.

He called out, "Lassie?" Then louder, as if she would materialize out of one of the shelves. Hardly. She wouldn't have climbed up the ladder, so that just left one place she could be. The tunnel.

And the tunnel ended on the cliff edge.

The Morning Star

Back into the rain, he thought wearily. *At least I hadn't dried off yet.* Then he was ashamed to be worrying about getting wet when his dog . . .

He choked back a rising sob. Without turning on his flashlight, Jimmy half ran, stumbling against the stone walls, down the tunnel.

The wet afternoon light filled his eyes. He pulled up on the edge of the cliff, heart pounding, prayers shrieking around his head like piñon jays.

Below him, soft, liquid words rose up the cliff. He crouched and peered down. The river dizzily soared below. But wait, closer, much closer was that old man on a stone ledge. Lassie stood with him, looking solid, vibrant, alive. Thank God.

"Lassie!" The name burst from Jimmy's lips. She tipped her head up, looked at him, and barked.

Looked at him? He caught his breath. No, she turned to his voice like a gyroscope aligning itself.

The old man smiled up at him, a few of his teeth missing, but all his wrinkles relaxed into such a friendly expression that Jimmy wondered how in the world he had been afraid of this man.

Jimmy eagerly began to climb down to them. Little stones and clots of mud fell, spattering the ledge. The old man shook his head and held up his palm—wait.

So Jimmy backed up onto the path and waited, the rain falling like tiny drumbeats. The man, his long hair wound with a leather thong, bent over and talked softly to Lassie. She whined and began moving forward, anxious to reach Jimmy, but something about the old man halted her.

Slowly the man and dog climbed off the ledge, away from Jimmy and out of his sight. He restlessly paced the path, waiting. Finally he paced farther than before and saw them climbing up a trail he hadn't noticed. It was lined on both sides with large rocks. The old man went from one to the next, one hand on them as he walked. *Safe as a banister staircase,* Jimmy thought. But standing at the tunnel entrance, standing anywhere but practically on top of the trail, you couldn't even see the path.

That is also how the canyon is, Jimmy thought, his gaze on the man's curved back, on Lassie's plumed tail, waving in the rain. You can't see your way almost until you're there.

Isn't that how God is too? he thought. You can't see

where you're going until you begin. God shows you just a little at a time. Jimmy's gaze rested on the snarling brown ribbon of water below. If you saw too much of the trail, you might lose heart and refuse to go any farther.

Lassie pranced up to Jimmy. He stroked her and waved his hand before her eyes. She laughed up at him, blinking each time his hand crossed her face.

Blinking.

Jimmy did it again and again. She blinked, and sneezed at him him as if to say, Enough! Then she licked his chin.

"How did she, I mean, she can—" he began and stopped, looking up at the old man who grinned wide at him.

"But how?" Jimmy asked.

The man shrugged his shoulders and touched his lips, then his ears. He shrugged again. He didn't know Jimmy's words.

Maybe Karina could speak his language. "Do you know Navajo? Spanish?" he asked.

The man still shook his head, not understanding.

Jimmy held out his hand. Then the man came to him. As Jimmy led him into the tunnel, he remembered that this kiva was the old man's and that Jimmy was inviting the man to his own sacred ceremony center. That seemed rude, but he didn't know what else to do. He hoped the old man would forgive him if he were being impolite.

Jimmy had a feeling the man was forgoing many of his customs, his feelings and convictions even, for Lassie's sake.

They entered the main room. Lassie barked and Karina sat up, rubbing her eyes. "What's going on?" she asked sleepily, then saw the older man.

She sat up straight and addressed him in another language. The man shook his head.

"He doesn't speak Navajo," said Karina. "Maybe Spanish." She asked him something.

The old man answered in a broken way, not fluent.

Sarah was sitting up, looking wildly at Jimmy. He knew she was thinking of Kachinas.

"It's okay," he said to her. "He's a friend. Lassie had gone outside and he helped bring her back." He didn't know how to explain that Lassie could see again, so he said nothing for the moment.

Karina heated water in a pan and served each of them hot coffee in a tin mug. Even Sarah drank it, making faces, but not arguing about how bitter it tasted.

The old man sipped his coffee with pleasure as he and Karina talked back and forth.

"I sure feel like an outsider," said Sarah.

"I know what you mean," Jimmy said. Yet he knew Karina would tell them what she and the man were saying when she had a chance. It was funny that Karina talked of not belonging, but he could see how much she did belong to this canyon world, much more than he did, more than he ever would.

Finally Karina said to them in English, "His Spanish isn't real good and my Hopi is really poor, but I think he's telling us that he has been watching Lassie ever since we came to the canyon. He thinks she is beautiful. He's been intrigued because he's seen old drawings of her on rocks."

"Old drawings of Lassie?" exclaimed Sarah. "How old? The last time we were here was last summer. Did someone draw Lassie then? But why?"

Karina shook her head. "He means old drawings like the ones on rocks. It sounds unbelievable, but I think he wanted to help her because his ancestors had dogs like her."

"Lassie's ancestors are from Scotland," said Sarah. "The British Isles. Her pedigree shows that. We have the papers."

Karina shrugged. "I'm just repeating what he said."

Jimmy asked, "Did he say anything about Lassie's eyes?"

Karina asked the old man.

He grew animated, waving his hands, pointing to his eyes, Lassie's eyes, then waving a circle around them.

Karina gasped and made him repeat his words, his gestures. Then she got up. "I must be misunderstanding him," she said.

"I don't think so," said Jimmy happily. "She can see again."

"What? Who? How?" demanded Sarah.

Karina passed her hand before Lassie's eyes. The dog blinked. Karina fished a piece of beef jerky out of the pack and tossed it. Lassie caught the morsel in midair and gobbled it. "She can see again," said Karina amazed.

Jimmy said, "Would you tell him thank you?" Then his throat constricted and he had to sternly tell himself not to cry.

Karina did. The old man turned to Jimmy and said something to Jimmy in Hopi. Karina puzzled over it while Jimmy waited impatiently to understand. Surely the old man had some terrific medical cure. Would he tell them what it was?

Karina and the old man went back and forth in Spanish and Hopi. The two languages were so different. One was melodic, the other more prickly, harsher sounding like the desert itself.

Finally Karina took a deep breath, "He says that your *Taláwsohu* healed Lassie."

"My what?" exclaimed Jimmy.

"*Taláwsohu*. It's Hopi for the star that shines as the sun comes up. You know, the morning star."

My morning star? Jimmy puzzled over that, then suddenly as if he were back in Sunday school, he could hear the class reciting Jesus' many names. Counselor. Bread of life. The Way. The Morning Star. Jesus was the Morning Star.

Indian Collie

There was no way Jimmy could ever return what the old man had given him. All he could think to ask was, "Is he hungry? We can fix something here."

Karina asked, and the old man answered, "Bah!"

Jimmy didn't need a translation for that! He didn't blame the guy for not wanting their freeze-dried stuff.

The old man got up and walked out. Boy, he really didn't want their cooking!

"He went to get us food," said Karina.

"I wanted to do something for him," protested Jimmy.

"I think he sees us as his guests," said Karina.

"What's his name?" asked Sarah.

"Ramon. That's his Spanish name. He said he told his Hopi name to Lassie."

Jimmy chuckled. "He sure likes you, Lassie." He threw his arms around his dog. "I can't believe she can see."

"I can," said Sarah. "I prayed God would heal her. He takes pretty good care of her, doesn't He?"

Karina watched their exchange with an amused glint in her eyes. "We, too, care much for our animals, both domesticated and wild ones." Jimmy found when Karina referred to herself as "we," she meant the Navajo and Hopi part of her. Or was it a part? Could you really divide yourself up?

Jimmy walked back out through the tunnel. Rain still pattered down. The rivers would be getting bigger. How would they get out?

But as he stood in the entrance of the tunnel, his anxiety flowed away. Lassie regaining her sight was so tremendous, how could he think that God wasn't helping them? Obviously God had a plan that included the rivers running wild.

Jimmy stood watching the clouds. Up from the cliffs came a figure. Of course, it was the man. But something large covered his head. Jimmy froze. Not after all this, a Kachina?

The man slowly trudged up the trail. Jimmy let out a breath. Of course, it was Ramon, but he carried a large basket on his head.

That's what he'd seen last night. Not a Kachina after all. He could kick himself for being spooked.

What kind of Christian am I? he wondered. *I pray, thank God, then instantly am terrified. I must have no faith.*

Then he thought, *I'm a normal Christian.* That's what Dad always says. It's normal to act human, to be scared, irritated, whatever. But it's superhuman to be like Christ, and it takes the Spirit to change you.

Jimmy stepped into the rain and down the trail. He took some short, heavy logs from Ramon, then they ducked inside. Ramon fixed an excellent meal with a thin corn bread called *piki,* and rabbit stew with beans and vegetables.

Sarah had shrieked, "rabbit!" But she'd eaten it and even asked for seconds. Lassie stretched out beside Ramon during the meal. He fed her choice bits of meat. Later Ramon gave her more herbs while Jimmy watched. Jimmy asked about the herbs, but Karina's verbal skills with Ramon broke down.

After much talking and drawing leaves on the ground in the sand, Karina said, "I don't know enough Hopi and he doesn't know the Spanish names for the plants. He just keeps saying, 'It's good medicine.' "

"I guess so!" replied Jimmy.

As they talked in their triangle of communication with gestures and quick, sand sketches, Karina asked Ramon about a way over the river. His white eyebrows lifted in what? Disbelief? Karina and Ramon talked on.

"What? What does he say?" Jimmy asked impatiently.

Karina shook her head. "He says he'll show us in the morning. Something about a . . ." she touched her fingers together, like he had, "a bridge, I guess. But I've never heard of one." She caught Jimmy's eye. "I think I'm understanding him correctly."

Jimmy hoped she was, too. If Ramon had said he had

a star ship for them to fly in, Jimmy would just about believe him.

That night Ramon stayed with them, and Jimmy found himself relaxed and able to fall asleep easily.

Early in the morning, Ramon woke them all. He had made them breakfast. Lassie gobbled down more rabbit stew. Then they packed the little stuff they had. Ramon carefully covered the fire. Not to put it out, but to allow it to smoulder. So Jimmy knew he was right; Ramon lived in the kiva at least some of the time.

They went out through the tunnel. The world was gray, but the rain had stopped, temporarily at least.

Ramon led them, Lassie at his heels, down along a cliff trail toward the mouth of the canyon where base camp was. Jimmy walked last with Sarah directly in front of him. He wished they were roped together. What if she tripped?

He worried for nothing, as he was discovering a lot of his worry was for nothing. She didn't trip. None of them did. Ramon walked quickly, lightly, not like an old man, and they followed in his wake like baby quail or chicks.

After a good hike, they veered up a steep grade, scrambling over thick tree roots. Behind the trees was a boulder the size of a school bus.

Paintings were strung across it.

"Oh," said Karina in perfect shock. "Look at this. Dr. Harmon would love to see this." She snatched out her camera and began shooting pictures like mad.

Ramon stood back, chuckling under his breath, like an art gallery owner. Lassie sat at his feet, content.

Jimmy drew close and realized they weren't only paintings, but most of them were actually chipped into the stone.

Karina ran her fingers over the stone, murmuring jargon words to herself like, "Patina formation" and "petroglyphs."

Jimmy just stared at the artwork—the pieces of corn, the flock of birds, the stick-like people and hand prints.

Sarah laughed and said, "I can draw better than that!"

Some of the drawings did look as if a kindergartner had gone nuts. But some of the others, even though they were simple, had a certain elegance that Jimmy doubted Sarah could have drawn.

From the far side of the boulder, Karina called, "Here's your ancient collie."

Jimmy and Sarah hurried to look at what Karina had found. They saw a square-bodied man with what looked like seashells around his neck and a fingerless, round hand on a dog's head. However, the dog was less simple. Pricked ears that tipped down on the ends rose from the slender, cone-shaped muzzle. Its legs were long and the tail waved with collie-like feathers. The chipped stone held faint painted pigment, brown, tan, black. Collie colors.

It was an Indian collie.

23

The Canyon of the Heart

Karina shot a photo of the collie art with Lassie sitting beside it and Jimmy on the other side. "No one will believe it," she kept saying.

"I think maybe it's really a hairy goat," teased Sarah.

Jimmy tossed a pebble at her. Sarah caught it and threw it back.

When they were done examining the drawings, Ramon led them farther along the cliff face. Lassie, who had been following close behind Ramon, suddenly scampered up a faint side trail and stood on a ledge, as if daring someone to come get her.

"You rascal," said Jimmy. He lightly scrambled up after her. Clouds still hung over the canyon, but rays of sunlight jetted in like beams from powerful lights.

Jimmy looked with awe over the canyon. "Better than a stage show," he told Lassie. She barked, and her voice bounced off the opposite canyon wall.

"What are you doing?" called Karina.

"I don't know," replied Jimmy. "Lassie's enjoying the view, I guess."

"Maybe she thinks there's another dog across the canyon," said Sarah.

Jimmy made a face. "She isn't that dumb."

A ray of sunlight beamed over the opposite canyon cliff. For a moment Jimmy just stared, unbelieving. He rubbed his eyes and gawked.

A city was built in the overhang of the opposite canyon wall. Not just a tower, a couple of storage rooms, or a stray kiva, but dozens of rooms, many built on top of each other.

Jimmy said in a strained voice, "Come up here, Karina."

"Now what?" Sarah muttered, but shoes scraped the trail and Karina joined him.

She looked anxiously at Lassie. "What's wrong?"

"Nothing. Look." He pointed. The sunlight still lit up the lost city like a searchlight. Karina gasped. Without looking she pulled out her camera and steadily shot pictures.

Once Jimmy glanced down at Ramon, and he was smiling a little. Sarah climbed up after them to look, too.

Soon the winds stirred up the clouds, the strong ray of light vanished, and the city in the cliff faded.

"No wonder we didn't see it before," said Karina as they were walking again along the trail after Ramon. "That overhang is huge. Dr. Harmon will be mad that he missed this. I wonder if anyone has explored it before."

Sarah snorted. "The people who lived there."

"She means archeology types," said Jimmy.

Jimmy half listened as Karina tried to get information out of Ramon about the city, but all he would say was that it was an old city of high houses. Karina had to be satisfied with that. She patted her camera. "At least I got photos," she said. "It's incredible."

The path turned south, and they were above the wash that had blocked their way. Here the two rivers met and crashed together in a giddy explosion of foaming water.

They climbed a steep stone staircase, slick from the rain. Footholds had been cut into the very cliff. Using their hands to help pull themselves up, except for Lassie who fairly skipped along, they struggled up.

The winds tore at Jimmy's hair the higher they climbed. A hawk blew past. The pit of his stomach grew queasy for a moment, like it did when he and his friend Blake had gotten tickets for a football game and they had been at the very top of an outdoor stadium.

They were on a pinnacle high above the wash, and across the wash, equally as high, was another pinnacle.

"It's like an old arch," said Karina. "You know, like you see at Window Rock and Arches National Park, only the top of the arch is missing."

"No, it's not," said Jimmy.

Ramon causally stood on two wooden timbers next to

one another that stretched the fifty feet from one pinnacle to the other. That was the bridge.

Sarah gripped Jimmy's arm. "We're supposed to walk on that!" she exclaimed.

Ramon said in a reassuring tone, "Okay, okay."

Even Karina looked a little squeamish. "It doesn't look okay," she said.

Jimmy thought, *If you trust someone, you trust them the whole way, otherwise what is the point?* He'd already trusted Ramon with Lassie, with himself, and with the others. Just because this looked frightening, did that mean it wasn't something he should do?

"It's okay, Sarah," Jimmy said. "I'll go first. You'll see."

"Be careful, Jimmy," Sarah begged, clutching his arm.

Jimmy drew closer. The wind was fierce. He almost had to lean into it so it wouldn't knock him off balance. The timbers were lashed together. Then he noticed something unusual. The timbers were curved, but curved inward, so the higher edges were on the outside of the timbers. It would be like walking down the middle of a long narrow bowl or inside a canoe. He could do that, couldn't he?

So he did. He didn't allow himself to look anywhere but at his feet and the path before him. The wind tore at him. One step. Two steps. Three steps. He counted under his breath. Despite the cold wind, sweat ran down his back. His mouth went dry as if he'd sucked sand for breakfast.

But he kept walking and the arch was firm.

Jimmy reached solid stone. He resisted falling on the ground and kissing it. When he turned to wave happily at the others, he nearly tripped over Lassie. She was there, at his heels.

"The whole time Lassie was right behind you, like she was connected to you," Karina told him after they had all safely crossed the arch.

"That wasn't so bad," said Sarah. "I wasn't scared after all."

Jimmy almost laughed in her face. "Want to do it again?"

"No, thanks," she said hastily. Then he did laugh.

Ramon carefully led them down the winding stone stairs on the other side. How the Anasazi worked! They had cut the steps and smoothed those stones hundreds of years ago.

The trail looked familiar now and they entered the peach orchard. "This is where I first saw Ramon," said Jimmy.

Ramon said something and Karina translated. "He said he let you see him here because he had a feeling we'd need his help later."

"How did he know?" asked Sarah.

"We consider him a holy man," said Karina. "They just seem to know these things."

Jimmy started to say thank you when Ramon disappeared somewhere between the peach trees.

They all looked at one another until Jimmy finally said, "Let's get back."

When they reached base camp, Uncle Cully and the students were just getting ready to leave to meet them at the river again.

"How in the world . . ." began Uncle Cully, but then he merely crushed Jimmy and Sarah to his chest. "It's so good to see you two. I was really worried."

"God is always with us, Uncle Cully," Jimmy said. "I keep having to remind you."

"Oh, I know," said Uncle Cully. "I just kept thinking how I was going to explain this to your mom and dad."

They broke camp the next morning and headed to Owenses' Ranch. Rain spat down at them and the clouds rode fast through the sky. Decker had been apologizing over and over since last night. Too much. Jimmy wanted him to just be quiet. It was okay.

Decker rode one of the mules, lightly packed, and Karina rode his ugly brown horse, letting Triangle follow without any weight on her back. She still favored her knee, but the swelling was nearly gone.

Jimmy and Karina rode side by side with Lassie bounding beside them. Uncle Cully had been amazed at the collie's healing.

"You should have asked Ramon for herbs for Triangle," said Jimmy.

Karina cocked her head. "I thought you believed Jesus healed Lassie."

"I think it was both," said Jimmy. "A lot of times God uses what He has already given us—like doctors and . . ."

"And herbs," Karina added.

"And herbs to help with healing," Jimmy said.

Karina pointed a finger at him. "Trying to trap me into saying I believe what you believe?"

"No, I'm not!"

"What are you two talking about?" asked Petra.

"We're talking about what we can believe in," said Karina.

Jimmy smiled. "The word is *faith*, and I think that Ramon and Lassie taught me a lot about faith these last couple of days."

"Me, too," said Karina, softly. A warmth stole over Jimmy. He knew Karina was close to seeking that personal Friend she could trust.

Jimmy shifted on Geometry's back—his legs were still sore! In the excitement he had forgotten to show Ramon the strange stones he found at the beginning of the trip. He looked back. The canyon was already lost in the folds of desert, but it was forever embedded in his mind's eyes. The funny thing was, he knew he'd be back and he knew the canyon would be waiting there to show him more secrets of life. He hoped that he'd see Ramon again.

"Race you!" Jimmy suddenly shouted and clapped his heels into Geometry's side. Karina and Lassie shot across the desert after him, shouting and laughing.

Author's Note

The Hopi are a private people, even more so lately because erroneous materials have been published about them. They are a part of our country's heritage and I think it is important to look at history in its entirety. My intention has not been to show disrespect, but to help educate. I wanted children to know about the wonders of the desert world that God created, and for me that should include the Hopi people. My respect for the Hopi and the Anasazi is great.

Echo Cliffs, Little Lizard Canyon, and the ruins on this journey are made-up, but I was true to the New Mexican desert and mountains and her incredible Anasazi ruins. The Cebolleta Mountains are real.

For more information about the Hopi people, the Anasazi Indians, and the New Mexican desert, check your local public library for the following titles:

ANCIENT WALLS: INDIAN RUINS OF THE SOUTHWEST
by Chuck Place; Fulcrum Publishing, 1987 (great photos)

GRANDMOTHER'S ADOBE DOLLHOUSE
by MaryLou M. Smith; illustrated by Ann Blackstone; New Mexico Magazine, 1984 (picture book)

KIDS EXPLORE THE HERITAGE OF WESTERN NATIVE AMERICANS
by Westridge Young Writers Workshop; John Muir Publications, 1995 (stories, crafts, games by Indian kids)

Marian Bray